A FLOWERING WOUND

A Flowering Wound

by

John Howard

The Swan River Press
Dublin, Ireland
MMXIX

A Flowering Wound
by John Howard

Published by
The Swan River Press
Dublin, Ireland
in July, MMXIX

www.swanriverpress.ie
brian@swanriverpress.ie

Stories © John Howard, MMXIX

"After the Earthquake"
© Erica Mann Jong, 1977, 1991.
Used by permission of the poet.

Dust jacket design by Meggan Kehrli
from cover artwork by Jason Zerrillo

Set in Garamond by Ken Mackenzie

Published with support from Dublin UNESCO
City of Literature and Dublin City Libraries

ISBN 978-1-78380-027-8

A Flowering Wound
is limited to 300 copies.

Contents

A Glimpse of the City 7

Portrait in an Unfaded Photograph . . . 28

The Golden Mile 48

Falling Into Stone 62

Ziegler Against the World 76

A Flowering Wound 102

We, the Rescued 110

The Man Ahead 134

Twilight of the Airships 147

Under the Sun 168

Acknowledgements 187

For Mat Joiner

A Glimpse of the City

You walk your whole life long
on a thousand streets;
on your way you see
those who forgot you.
An eye beckons,
the soul tingles;
you found it
only for seconds . . .
Two strange eyes, a quick glance,
the brows, pupils, the lids;
What was that? No-one turns time back . . .
Gone with the wind, passed, nevermore.

– Kurt Tucholsky, *Eyes in the City*

Clemens and I had been to a book launch at the New National Gallery. Clemens moves around a lot in Berlin's artistic circles, and I can never resist the chance to join him at one of the free handouts of wine and canapés that are usually provided at their events. Also I like to take every opportunity I can to get networking and try to grow the one-man translation business that is me and which seems to occupy most of my waking hours. At the launch I had, I hoped, made some useful future contacts. With the money I make from my work and the income Clemens gets from his journalism and freelance writing,

A Glimpse of the City

between us we get along all right. At any rate, we can pay the rent on our large, cool flat high up in one of the long Stalinist wedding-cake blocks along Karl-Marx-Allee, and still have a few euros left at the end of each week.

Felix, the photographer whose book had just been launched into the world, is one of Clemens' oldest friends. He had presented us with a boxed copy of the new book. Somehow I kept it with me all through the afternoon; it was like trying to hold a paving slab under my arm. I dreaded what would happen if it slipped—it'd probably cripple me for life if it fell on one of my feet.

We were both feeling pleasantly light-headed as we wandered away from the New National Gallery. It was a warm Friday afternoon. With the approaching weekend the rush-hour had started early. In Potsdamer Strasse the dusty air was full of traffic fumes. Sunlight glinted off windscreens. Swarms of office workers and construction and maintenance workers finishing earlier than usual increased the sense of being hemmed in on pavements already crowded with tourists and visitors heading to the Kulturforum.

"Let's walk for a bit," Clemens said.

"You can carry this bloody book then," I replied. "It weighs a ton. I keep thinking I'm going to drop it."

Clemens laughed. "Ah, don't be complaining so much, Paul! It's a lovely big free book for you. All those artistic photos around Berlin and its people. You will love it."

There he was almost certainly right—annoyingly. Clemens is a native Berliner, from the former Eastern part of the city. He never tired of talking about the changes he'd seen; and I never tired of listening to him. Berlin utterly fascinated me right from my first visit; only my own native city, London, has exercised a comparable hold over me. But Clemens had come back to Berlin, and therefore so had I.

A Flowering Wound

Clemens squeezed my bicep. "Hard. Lots of strength there," he laughed. Then he squeezed again. It hurt. I nearly did drop the book; sometimes that man didn't know his own strength. Clemens had stopped walking; his grip on my arm relaxed just enough to stop it hurting, but not so much that I could shake free and continue to walk. I took one step back, and stood beside him. He stepped over to the inside of the pavement, still holding my arm lightly and pulling me with him. We stood facing into the flow of most of the people crowding it.

"Paul, look ahead, coming towards us. No, don't stare. Just look."

"What at? Where? Oh. Oh. I see . . . "

Clemens released his grip on my arm, and then nudged it. Pain flared up again for a moment; I shoved the book at him, but he wouldn't take it. He was still looking as well. "Hey Paul, that's what you come to Berlin for, isn't it?"

By then he'd brushed past us. But I'd seen enough. He was a young man—very young, perhaps only nineteen or so—not tall, but with broad shoulders and a torso tapering down to a narrow waist. He wore close-fitting blue overalls unbuttoned far enough to reveal a wide chest under a white T shirt. The sleeves of his overalls were rolled up, showing muscular arms. A rucksack or equipment bag was slung over one shoulder. Under long eyelashes he had the most intense dark brown eyes that I'd ever seen. He was a dark-complexioned man, with very short black hair and a mouth like a barely opened bud. His look of almost ferocious concentration was like a wave riding in advance of him as he made his way through the crowd.

I started to turn, to follow him with my eyes. Perhaps I thought he would look back and smile. Clemens grasped my arm again.

9

A Glimpse of the City

"No, don't look back, Paul. Your heart will be captured. He might steal your soul, one like that. I will not look back!"

I looked back anyway. I couldn't see any sign of him, not even the back of those wide blue-clad shoulders with the rucksack swinging easily as he walked away from us. The man had disappeared into the crowd.

"He is a real worker, I reckon," Clemens said. "But not a dirty one, you know? He has a nicer job, maybe he is something like an electrician, yes? It's too early to get dressed up like that and be going to a gear fetish club!"

"Don't spoil the moment," I said. "You don't see someone like that every day. But I wouldn't say no to the chance to."

"Paul, like I say, you came to Berlin to see men like that," Clemens said.

"No, it was because of you . . . but . . . "

We started walking again. The book still weighed me down.

"Let's have a beer before going home," Clemens said. He laughed again.

"Yeah, fine."

⁂

It wasn't far to one of our regular bars, a place just off Leipziger Platz. It wasn't very atmospheric: it was too new for that. The marble and chrome was still too shiny, but the air-conditioning worked and it was fairly quiet. A few refugees from the book launch showed up not long after we had sat down with our chilled beers. We all nodded at each other, and they passed on by.

I'd placed Felix's book on the low glass table between us. Clemens leaned over and lifted one side of it.

"Wow, yes, that is a heavy book," he said. "I will carry it home the rest of the way."

"Thanks very much!"

A Flowering Wound

"But first I will have a look. We are in no hurry are we, Paul?"

"No. It's your turn to cook, remember."

I finished my beer and went to the bar to get two more. When I got back Clemens had the book open, and was slowly turning the pages, leafing through it intently as if searching for a particular picture.

"You will not believe what I have found, all by accident, here in this book," he said. "Sit down. Have a look."

Clemens grimaced as he hoisted the book off his knees and back onto the table. He rested it on top of its box, which promptly collapsed flat under the weight. He swivelled the book around so it faced me. I liked Felix Huber's photographs from the moment I had first seen them. They were nearly always in black and white; and for me they summed-up the essence of modern Berlin in the same way that Hermann Rückwardt's photographs from the late nineteenth century did for Imperial Berlin. Although Felix often used a tried and trusted film camera, developing the photos himself, his gifts extended beyond that and into making imaginative use of digital photography and image-editing software. In his work Felix did much more than just put on display gritty and detailed personal statements of today's city. Once, he had exhibited a sequence of photographs in which contemporary Berlin was bodied-forth in grey and sepia homages to all the atmosphere and character of the old. I always remembered in another group Felix had combined old and new images in a surreal mixing: long-destroyed buildings from the Imperial era stood next to, within, and outside their successors. People from the different centuries caught in the photos, whether involuntarily or posing, were swallowed up into human and stone montages that spanned decades and mixed frozen attitudes and expressions, shadows cast, trees and cloud formations. Felix had used old photographs, postcards, slides, even

A Glimpse of the City

pieces of still film. The result was a Berlin not fully on this plane of existence—which appealed to me, as that was how I liked to think of the city anyway.

"What have you found?"

"This one. See." Clemens tapped one of the photos on the page.

I leaned forwards over the open book. After a moment I recognised part of the interior of Friedrichstrasse Station. The accompanying text stated that the photo had been taken the previous year. Sunlight, stopped in its own tracks, slanted down from the glass roofs and onto the kiosks and railway tracks. The heads of the people standing together on the platform were like marbles. I scanned the photo for whatever it was that had caught Clemens' attention. Then I saw. It was the young man we'd seen earlier. Or if it wasn't him it was an identical twin or a stunning double; and the streets of Berlin had just become even more alluring.

"He doesn't look any different, does he?" I said.

"Maybe he is forever young. That would be something!"

❧

All around us our apartment settled into the long evening. After dinner we padded through to the sitting room. The floor was cool under my bare feet, the slightly uneven wooden blocks brown as chocolate. The balcony doors were open; the vast hush of Karl-Marx-Allee flowed up and into the room. Clemens brought the wine through and sat down next to me on the sofa. I pulled the book onto my lap. It made me appreciate why coffee table books were called that. I turned back to the beginning and started to look at each photograph in turn. Clemens switched on the television to watch a film—I paid no attention as I was soon fully absorbed in Felix Huber's work—but he occasionally leaned

A Flowering Wound

over and looked at the page I was examining. He also kept my wineglass filled.

Brilliant light suddenly fell over the page and pooled there, reflecting in the glossy paper. Clemens had turned the light on: I hadn't realised that it was now twilight outside and I must've been gradually leaning forward, peering ever closer at the photographs. Perhaps it was a coincidence that I saw the young man again on the next page I turned. This time he was in one of a group of photographs taken during the restoration of the Bell Tower and Langemarck Hall at the Olympic Stadium. It was certainly the right environment for him. He was standing in a group of men who were all wearing overalls and safety helmets, and holding screwdrivers, hammers, power drills, bundles of wire. The workers grinned for the camera; but I could make out that although the young man was smiling, he didn't seem to be looking at the camera. He stood with his arms folded across his chest, shoulders thrown back. His eyes were not looking directly forward as his co-workers were, but off to one side, apparently towards one of the massive metal girders that underpinned and rooted the structure. They had not been allowed to be visible from the outside; only the appearance of solid granite had been considered suitable.

Clemens said, "He is looking exactly the same there, too. That photo must be five or six years old."

I got up and crossed over to the balcony door. Outside, the air was cool and fresh. To the west the Television Tower was a black sliver against a band of primrose sky. I turned back and returned to the sofa. Clemens had switched off the television. We sat down again and finished the bottle of wine.

"Do you know what I want to do now?" I said.

"Try me," Clemens said. "But we're not going out to Jens' Bar. Those guys might be there again. Remember? They were some strange guys."

A Glimpse of the City

I put my hand on his knee and shook my head. "I was going to be serious for a moment! I don't know why I'm thinking this way, getting interested in that man. But I now want to go through all the other books of Berlin photos that we've got and look for him. I'm sure I'll find him in some more pictures. Now I know what he looks like. But I know it's stupid."

"Listen, maybe you could look in those books tomorrow, Paul? We haven't got anything planned. But right now, I just want to go to bed."

"It's still quite early."

"Exactly. You always said you liked the way I could call out your name using three, what is the word, syllables?"

❧

Saturday morning was warm and sunny. We opened windows and the balcony door. The fountain in Strausberger Platz had been turned on. Later it would catch the sun and turn into thin strips of glittering foil shaking in a breeze. Our breakfasts at weekends were always leisurely and almost choreographed, a series of events in which we both took our self-assigned parts. I made the coffee (a more expensive one than usual as it was the weekend) and set out the table, loading it with sliced cheeses, tubs of cream cheese, thinly-cut ham and salami, pots of jam, sliced cucumbers, gherkins, yoghurt, and fruit. Clemens went down to the bakery in the arcade on the ground floor to buy fresh warm rolls. Saturday morning breakfast was my favourite time of the week. In summer we opened the kitchen window and let in the sounds rising up from the back of the block: car engines being started and revved up; the clanging of rubbish being thrown into the communal bins; neighbours calling to each other; children shouting and screaming as

A Flowering Wound

they ran in and out of the back entrance passageways and doors. From where I sat I could see the grimy brown brick tower of a church and the tops of the trees in the cemetery. I switched on the radio and selected one of the local music and chat stations.

Clemens put a large paper bag full of rolls down on the table. I poured out glasses of orange juice and cups of coffee. On Saturday mornings we usually discussed plans for the rest of the weekend as we relaxed into our free time. In practice our times for working and leisure weren't so clearly defined: there had been times when I'd spent a Sunday revising a translation, or Clemens had been forced to spend most of a Saturday sitting at his computer working on an article when a deadline had changed. And at other times we'd find ourselves, in compensation, with a couple of free afternoons in the middle of the week. But I'd already decided what I wanted to do on this Saturday.

"You are going to look through your books of photos, then?" Clemens said. "It is such a wonderful sunny day. We could go to the beach at Wannsee."

"Along with thousands of others," I replied. "Clemens, you can go if you like. I want to check out the photos. I've got that feeling. You know what I'm like when I get going on something."

"Yes, you can be very intense."

"That's the way it is." I smiled at Clemens and reached for his hand, but he'd picked up his mug and was gulping down the last of his coffee.

We cleared away the breakfast things, and I went into the spare bedroom, which we'd converted into a workroom where we both had our desks and computers. By my desk there was a bookcase full of dictionaries and grammar books, guidebooks and collections of photos, and a whole shelf of histories of Berlin and any number of old maps

A Glimpse of the City

and street atlases that I'd picked up over the years. I found Felix Huber's previous books, and added some collections of reproductions of old postcards to the pile. Then I took them through to the living room.

The windows and open balcony door were glaring rectangles of light, divided into halves of blazing blue sky and dull grey stone. It was already getting hot outside. The block opposite to ours was in deep shadow. From our height Karl-Marx-Allee was a calm and almost deserted canyon of stone, concrete, and tarmac. Cars were toys, flashing as they moved out of shadow and caught the sun. The room was cool and dim.

I started working my way down through the ziggurat of books I'd piled on the floor. I turned pages slowly, leaning over them or holding them close to my eyes as I minutely examined likely photographs. At some point a mug of coffee and a cake materialised on the table next to me. I looked up and saw Clemens' back disappearing through the doorway. A few moments later I heard the front door closing.

I saw the young man several books later, in a collection of photos covering the history of the Berlin Wall. It was unmistakeably him. There he was in the mid-1970s standing on a viewing platform on the western side of the Wall looking down into Sonnenallee, at what amounted to the international frontier at the boundary between the Berlin boroughs of Neukölln and Treptow. He stood at the front of a group of teenagers—possibly all from the same school class—waving at the East German border guards as they manned their checkpoint. Perhaps some daring East German boys and girls of their own age were waving back, out of the picture. The young man had his muscular arms folded in front of him; his shirt was unbuttoned, giving a tantalising hint of his broad chest. The body language implied that he and the teenagers were friends or at least contemporaries, but none of those next to him showed any sign of realising he was there. He could've been a block of concrete or a lamp post as far as they were concerned. I slipped a piece of paper between the pages to mark the place.

An hour or so later I found what turned out to be the second photograph (or third, if I counted the one in Huber's new book) containing the young man. This one was in a book on post-war Berlin and its reconstruction in the years before 1949. Much of the city had been reduced to shattered ruins and enormous piles of rubble. I examined photo after photo of a sterile cityscape of gutted apartment blocks and burnt-out public buildings. And yet life went on. People patched-up roofs and walls and grew vegetables in roofless rooms. The authorities needed to get the ruins cleared away so the rebuilding could begin; because the overwhelming majority of able-bodied men who had not been killed were still prisoners of war, the task of clearing away the rubble fell to women. They had soon been labelled rubble-women—the legendary *Trümmerfrauen*. Ruins were dismantled brick by brick; bricks were passed along the lines of women and girls, hand to hand. They were recovered, laboriously cleaned and stacked for reuse. Blocked streets reappeared and became passable again; tram routes were freed from mangled wreckage. And in a photograph of a group of *Trümmerfrauen* at work in the jumbled debris of the Kurfürstendamm, I saw him.

In the distance were the jagged ruins of the massive Kaiser Wilhelm Memorial Church, its shattered towers still soaring into the empty sky, marooned like a battleship in a dried-out harbour. Shadows were sharply defined: light and dark were clear in those hot summers of defeat. There was a line of women of all ages—some standing, and some sitting on stacks of bricks. They were hard at work; their expressions were as pinched as their bodies looked to be un-

A Glimpse of the City

der the rough clothes they wore. And off to one side stood the young man, not apparently taking any notice of the activity going on around him, but grinning at something that seemed to lie behind the camera. He squinted into the sun. His patched overalls couldn't disguise the fact that he was much thinner than I'd ever seen him; still muscular, but in a lean and wiry rather than bulky way.

I marked the page and put the book down on the floor. I'd had enough. Berlin's photographic history was swirling through my mind, and I was thirsty and had a slight headache. I was in the kitchen making a cup of tea when Clemens came in. His face and bare arms were sunburnt; against his scalp his fair hair seemed close to white. I looked at the clock: I could hardly believe that it was now the middle of the afternoon. I poured Clemens a cup of tea as well, and we sat down at the table.

"How have you been doing?" he asked.

"I'll show you. I've found him in two more photos. I might've missed some, but it's definitely him in two photos. And they're old photos, but he doesn't look any different. Clemens, I can't explain it."

"You are making a big obsession for yourself, I think, Paul."

"I'll show you the photos. And anyway, you were the one who first pointed him out to me. I might not have noticed him if you hadn't."

Clemens sipped his tea, deep in thought. "Or maybe you would have seen him anyway. Okay, you show me, a bit later."

"What have you done today?"

"Oh, I only went to the Tierpark. Then I had some lunch and a drink at the Ring-Center."

I burst out laughing. "You don't like animals!"

"No."

18

A Flowering Wound

❧

That evening we decided not to go out to a bar or club. After dinner we strolled to Friedrichshain Park and climbed to the top of the larger of the two hills that had been formed by covering the monstrous broken hulks of wartime flak towers with rubble and soil. We followed the curving paths. On the way I told Clemens about the two photos I'd discovered, and especially the older one. Near the summit of the hill we sat on a cracked concrete wall that was actually part of the damaged parapet of the flak tower. It was dusky under the trees. From the top we watched the sun sink into the horizon, a distorted orange ball in a burning swirl of wispy cloud. Lights started to blink on in the twilight. The city sank into a haze. We held hands as we walked back down.

In Strausberger Platz Clemens said, "Let's go drink Cuba Libres."

There was a bar in the ground floor arcade of the block next to ours. The bar's décor had been restored to what it would've been like when it was first decorated in the early 1950s. Although we usually drank beer and wine, Clemens did like to drink cocktails sometimes. I don't often drink spirits; but I also fancied a drink, and certainly didn't want to create any more problems by hesitating. After three Cuba Libres each I realised that I was talking a lot about the photos and the young man. I spoke rapidly. "At this rate I'll have to think about a suitable name to give him," I said. "I can't keep on calling him the young man. Or even the gorgeous young man. Which he is, you must agree."

"You talked a lot in this way at that party in London when we first met," Clemens said. "You were all enthusiastic then, as well."

"I'm sorry. I don't mean to go on about him."

"I know. It's just that . . . Well, all this . . . And maybe wanting to find a name for him? It is a bit funny, thinking about doing that." Clemens ordered another cocktail each. "These must be our last ones."

We sat in silence until the drinks arrived. Then Clemens said, "Paul, I have an idea. Maybe if you find him in some other photos as well, we can try to find out more about him. Solve this, sort of, mystery? Then we could maybe write something together. One of the Berlin magazines might be interested. We could even do it as a fiction story."

I smiled at Clemens and put my hand on his thigh. It wasn't only the Cuba Libres acting on me. Clemens and I had collaborated several times before: I'd interpreted at interviews and translated documents and passages from books to help Clemens with his research for articles. I had always been eager to get involved with his work. And we'd always laughed about it, telling our friends and Clemens' sympathetic colleagues that our collaborations were just an example of cementing international relations and one further illustration of the concept of euphemism. But this time I didn't answer him straight away.

"If that is how you are feeling," he said, as we got up to go home.

I didn't get to sleep until long after midnight. Like everybody who lives with anybody else, we have argued, disagreed, fallen out with each other, and retreated into sullen silences. Unlike some of our friends we have never split up before getting back together again; our settling of differences had always happened while living as a couple, just as the original problems—no matter how trivial or serious—had done. And when we've been at home together we never slept apart. I mean that our bodies always shared the same bed—even if every other part of us wanted to be somewhere else at the time. At the beginning we agreed we would try not to distance ourselves; we both knew the physical has its ways of reconciling the mental. Neither of us had ever regretted the result, even though some nights had been terrible, endless for one or both of us.

My hesitation had hurt Clemens, but I had needed to think about the consequences of what he had said. It was one thing for me to continue to look for a particular young man in old photographs, and no doubt look for him again on the street. I could imagine that on the following Friday afternoon at the same time, I would be at the same place, prepared and hopeful. Clemens' involvement somehow wasn't welcome, even though he'd started it all; but two rather than one would mean our security.

Clemens fell asleep before I did. I could tell. Once the warm contoured slopes of his back stopped moving, except for the gentlest motions of breathing and the reciprocal reaction of the bed, it was forbidden and impregnable. I faced the other way, making sure that nothing of me came into contact with any of him. That was the deal. I yawned and stretched, careful not to risk disturbing Clemens. I had hesitated, not because I wanted to indulge an obsession and pursue the young man, but because I didn't. Sure, perhaps I would look at him in the photos I had found and look for a few more. Whenever I saw a group of young workers near a construction or renovation site I would wonder if one of them could be him. But that would be it—nothing more than that, nothing serious. There was nothing at all for Clemens to get worried about, if only I could convince him. But of course I had to convince myself first, and stay convinced. I didn't want the responsibility of allowing the young man to penetrate any deeper into our lives than we

A Glimpse of the City

had already let him. I didn't want to pin him down, and so pin down Clemens and me as well. I didn't want us to advertise this fascination. And yet I felt that not pursuing it could be more threatening to us than pursuing it. I just had to explain my thoughts to Clemens. I thought about waking him up, but before I could I finally fell asleep as well. The next thing I knew it was early on Sunday morning: a normal one with the clanging of church bells blowing in through the wide-open windows, and fresh air and sunshine.

❧

Breakfast was subdued. We went through the motions. But we got through it. Later on Sunday mornings Clemens and I often liked to wander around a couple of flea markets. There were enough to choose from, each with widely different types of customer and sorts of things that could be found. Some flea markets were now well-known and a part of the regular tourist trail. They tended to be crowded and noisy, selling mainly worthless and uninteresting kitsch at high prices. Others were less-known outside their immediate neighbourhoods; and depending on who was selling, it was sometimes possible to buy some real bargains. Over the years I'd bought a large number of old guidebooks and maps; Clemens had a particularly good eye for glassware and coins. And neither of us minded having a go with a little haggling. During the previous week we'd already formed a tentative plan to go to the flea market near the Charlottenburg Gate. It was a big market, with several rows of stalls filling the car park and open space in front of the Ernst-Reuter-Haus. The market was a favourite with tourists, but also attracted Berliners from all parts of the city.

There was no need for any discussion. It was as if we both wanted to leave the previous day behind and return

A Flowering Wound

to the better circumstances of the working week now past. We took the U-Bahn to Alexanderplatz. "All lines lead to Alexanderplatz," Clemens said, as we negotiated the stairs and corridors to get to the platform for a Tiergarten train. He'd said that when I came to visit him in Berlin for the first time. I rested my hand on Clemens' shoulder for a moment.

"This reminds me of Felix's photo," Clemens said, as we waited for our train. Like Friedrichstrasse Station, the overground part of Alexanderplatz Station is basically a glass box open at both ends. It always gave me a feeling of light and air and freedom; of being slightly above and beyond the city streets, and able to travel. "Maybe your young man is here!"

Before I could answer the train pulled in. I always enjoyed travelling on the elevated section of the railway between Alexanderplatz and Charlottenburg Station. The journey was not long enough to get boring, and the line wound its way through and over much of the centre of Berlin. It was as if a distorted London had an overground railway built through it on brick arches from Paddington to the City, weaving through Hyde Park and Westminster close to Buckingham Palace, next to Trafalgar Square and along by the Strand, crossing the Thames twice, and running between the adjacent British Museum, National Gallery, and St. Paul's Cathedral.

Out in the open again the backs of apartment blocks were pockmarked grey cliffs. The city centre was impaled on the spike of the Television Tower. The Protestant Cathedral lumbered past the window, its swollen dome mobbed by birds. More passengers clambered on at Friedrichstrasse. Soon we glided past the Reichstag Building; each of its corner towers flew a flag almost as large as the tower itself. The golden goddess of the Victory Column floated over the trees, her wings frozen in place, silent. Next to the

A Glimpse of the City

river the train passed alongside more apartment buildings. Tiergarten Station was another bright and noisy glass and metal box.

We strolled up and down the crowded spaces between the lines of stalls. Clemens noticed a single pale-green *Jugendstil* wineglass isolated in a mass of modern mass-produced ones, and bought it without attempting to negotiate a lower price. I rummaged through a cardboard box heaving with books that had been set out on the ground next to the stallholder's table. Wedged in at one side I found a pocket-sized world atlas from the 1920s; a quick glance through the pages showed me that all the maps seemed to be there. I bought it for five euros.

Pleased with our purchases, we stopped at one of the stalls selling currywurst and beer and bought lunch. I was wiping some potato salad off my fingers when Clemens tapped me on the arm.

"Paul, look."

I followed Clemens' gaze. "I am not certain why I am telling you," he whispered.

I caught sight of the back of the young man's close-cropped head. His blue overalls were taut across his wide shoulders as he shoved his way past people browsing at a stall full of brassware and ironmongery. Ignoring Clemens, I started to follow the man, pushing through the teeming market and trying not to lose sight of him. We were heading towards the Charlottenburg Gate; the crowd was beginning to thin out towards the edge of the market. I was gradually getting closer to him, but I couldn't quite close the gap between us. I kept apologising as I bumped into people. Then he stopped at a table and turned round to face me. He stood with his legs apart, firmly planted on the tarmac, as if daring anyone to get in his way or try to move him. He folded his arms in front of his chest; his sleeves were rolled

A Flowering Wound

up, stretched over the muscles of his forearms. There was a day's growth of stubble on his unlined face: I wanted to reach out and run my smooth palm back and forth over its roughness. Then I was close enough to feel the absorbing gaze of his smouldering brown eyes. He broke into a grin. I started to smile back; and then he turned and began to run, forcing people to jump aside as he dashed past the last market stalls.

As I ran after him I heard Clemens trying to catch me up. He shouted "Paul, Paul!" Out of habit I started to turn and look at him, but then I put him out of my mind as I concentrated on trying to see where I was going. The young man had almost reached the Charlottenburg Gate. Clemens called out again. Perhaps it was my imagination but I thought the young man started to turn his head to look back, exactly as I had. He glanced back just once, very quickly. He was still grinning, and I saw his white teeth bared as he ran through one of the arches. When I reached the other side he had completely vanished. I stood there panting and sweating.

Clemens ran up to me. "Paul, what must we have looked like," he said. He was gasping for breath. "It is lucky for us no-one seems to have called the police. You could have been a thief I was chasing, or we were both chasing a bad man who had stolen something."

I leaned back against the archway. "Clemens, I'm really sorry," I said. "I don't know why I had to chase after him like that."

"I wonder if I know."

"Clemens—"

Then he bent over and picked something up from the pavement. "What is this?" he said. "He has dropped this."

Clemens handed me a wallet. It was made of brown leather, scuffed and cracked with age.

25

A Glimpse of the City

"You saw him drop it?"

"I am not sure. But you were worrying about something different."

"Let's see."

I opened the wallet and went through it, checking all the pockets and compartments. Tucked into one of the pockets I found a photograph; otherwise the wallet was empty. As I examined the photo I saw that it was actually half of a larger one that had been ripped down the middle. There were a couple of words scrawled on the back; when I turned the photo over it was with no surprise at all that I saw the young man. Although the photo seemed to be as old as the wallet was, he looked the same as I'd just seen him. He was shading his eyes with one hand as he gazed into the camera; he was leaning slightly towards the half of the photo that was missing. I handed it to Clemens.

"This man was with someone," he said carefully. "You can see it. They had a photograph of them made. Then maybe later they were not together anymore."

We found a bench and sat down. I gazed at the young man in the damaged photo. Clemens was right: at the torn edge of the photo I could make out a tiny piece of another shoulder and arm next to the young man's; a different fabric, maybe of a suit, next to his overalls. His nonchalant pose, legs apart; his open face, snapping eyes, short black hair and familiar grin; I felt warm breath and a sudden sharp emptiness. I held the photo but not him.

Clemens gently took the photo and turned it over. Then he held it out to me.

"It's just a name. There is just one name there now."

Paweł. That was the word scribbled on the back of the photo. "His name was Paweł," I said quietly. "All the time."

"I was at school with a boy called Paweł," Clemens said softly. "That name is the Polish version of Paul. There are a lot of people with Polish origins living in Berlin. But you know that."

I looked at the photograph again, held it up, close to my eyes. "*Ich bin Berliner*," I whispered. Then I tore up the photo and stuffed the pieces into the wallet. As we walked back to the station I threw the wallet in the first rubbish bin I noticed.

❧

Neither of us has seen Paweł since. In the photos where I had identified him the match now seems to be much less certain; the possibilities have faded. Once or twice now Clemens has speculated out loud that it's possible Paweł was not a proper Berliner, that his hair and complexion were perhaps too dark for him even to be a true German. (Clemens didn't say that my hair is black and that I don't have a fair complexion either.) I know his teasing and banter; and I love it. Our collaborations continue, with no end in sight. But there are moments when Clemens' charm and ability, his intelligence and urbanity, his Berlin-born acumen, his arresting blond hair, blue eyes and firm body—all of him and all his love for me—can seem to be a massive detour leading me out of my way. I even get anxious that I've taken a wrong turning somewhere, as if I'd wandered out of all regions familiar to me, away from my usual routes and into an unfamiliar street or district of the city.

Must there always be something or someone with the apparent potential to canker the bud?

Portrait in an Unfaded Photograph

*"Friendship based solely upon gratitude
is like a photograph; with time it fades."*

– Queen Elisabeth of Romania (Carmen Sylva)

On Assumption Eve

I, Gustav Meyer, now called Meyrink, of Peleş Castle, Sinaia, in Romania, and approaching the end of my life, will write down for the first time the true story of all that happened.

After three years or so at the bank I was still not very happy. The fact that I had co-founded the bank made no difference. My life seemed to have come to a dead end; I had wandered up a blind alley and there was no way forward. My literary ambitions, too, had not so far come to anything. It seemed to me that I was going to be both an unsuccessful writer and an unfulfilled banker.

Things came to a head on the day before the Feast of the Assumption, 14 August, in the year 1892. I had decided to solve all problems by removing myself from the scene. I purchased a gun, a small pistol, and took it home. I stood in the middle of my room next to my empty writing table, one hand on its edge, and with the other held the pistol against my head and waited to pull the trigger. Then I heard a rustling noise, and I was distracted enough to look towards

A Flowering Wound

the source: the door leading out of my room. I thought that perhaps a mouse was scuttling around, hunting here and there for something to eat. But there was no mouse to be seen. Instead, a small white rectangle rested on the worn carpet at the foot of the door. Clearly a piece of paper or card had been pushed under my door, and that was the sound I had heard.

Gently, I took the pistol away from my temple and put the pistol down on the table, while continuing to hold on to the table carefully. I walked slowly over to the door and picked up the object. It turned out to be a postcard, and I was looking at the reverse, which had no writing on it, no address; so how it got to be put under my door, and by whom, I could not guess. I jerked the door open, but there was nobody outside it. There was so sign of life, not even the back of my unknown postman receding down the corridor. There was no sound at all to be heard, no departing footsteps.

I turned the postcard over, and saw that it was a picture of a castle built in the style from old times, like the sort of place that the mad King Ludwig had been building in Bavaria before his death put an end to the construction activities that threatened to bankrupt the state. Turning the card over again, I noticed there was some writing after all: just the printed description of the picture, so small that it had been all too easy to overlook. The place was Peleş Castle in Romania, the summer residence of King Carol I and his Queen Consort, Elisabeth.

I remembered once reading something about the building of the castle, and dwelling on how much it was costing. (My banker's instinct had not been entirely wasted.) It was costing considerably less than what the late Bavarian monarch had been willing to spend on his buildings. Perhaps King Carol had more financial acumen than me or my

29

Portrait in an Unfaded Photograph

partner did. Or he was simply an astute man, intent on protecting his throne. Examining the picture further, I found that against my inclination, I was rather attracted to the castle. The setting looked idyllic: a place not quite of this world, made for escape and for openness to the restoring serenities of nature. The building itself, despite its obvious and impressive size and the use for which it had been built, still looked like a real home. The pistol lay forgotten on my table; a lump came to my throat as I thought about how pleasant it would be to travel to such a place and be able to stay there. A glass of dark beer was called for, and I locked the gun in the bottom drawer of my desk, slipped the postcard in my pocket, and went out into the busy street.

From that time onward I was intrigued. I tried to find out as much as I could about Peleş Castle and its royal inhabitants. I sought out articles in the popular magazines, and looked closely at the accompanying photographs. King Carol I: a minor German prince who had accepted the crown much-peddled around Europe by one of the many Brătianus or their friends who always seemed to be really running things in Romania. The King, with his bristling beard and piercing eyes, was stiff, serious, shrewd, upright. No duty was too much for him, and he was every inch a scion of the Hohenzollerns. And then his wife, the Queen, Elisabeth: such a contrast! Gentle and yet deeply determined; artistic, a dreamer and romantic; still yearning and suffering nearly twenty years after the death of her daughter at four years of age. The King did not seem to share his wife's sorrow. The Queen was always portrayed wearing long flowing gowns, and with an expression sensitive and somewhat mournful, seemingly having attained a sort of peace and repose. And indeed she was an artist. She drew, painted, and played several musical instruments; and she

A Flowering Wound

wrote. Of course! I remembered that she wrote all types of literary work—novels, stories, poems, essays—that she published under the name of Carmen Sylva.

Not only did I always keep the miraculous postcard of Peleş Castle safe in my wallet, but I also started carrying a selection of postcards of Carmen Sylva, and clippings about her and her works. At odd moments in my office at the bank, or on a tram, or in the street, or in my room, I would look upon her kindly face and feel that, despite all her own troubles and responsibilities, she would, if she but knew, shoulder a selection of mine, and perhaps transform them through her talents in the media of prose and verse.

This obsession—I must call it that—continued for two or three years. And then, as the bank continued to grow more deadly to me and I could make no progress with my literary work, I hit upon the solution. I berated myself for not thinking of it earlier. As I have explained, I had become an assiduous reader of articles about Queen Elisabeth and Peleş Castle, and also of the many artists she entertained there and supported in a variety of ways. If only I could receive an invitation to Peleş Castle! If only I could secure the Queen's patronage! I wrote her a letter, in which I opened my heart to her. Then I sat back and waited and waited. But no reply ever came.

To say that I felt betrayed, cheated, cast aside, would be the most absolute of understatements. In my gloom when I was feeling most rational, I thought that perhaps the King or his Prime Minister—who I knew visited the castle often for conferences with the King, and had official rooms maintained there—had been handed my letter, read it, and prevented the Queen from seeing it. Perhaps letters from her to me were being extracted from the postal system by the authorities of my own country, at the request of Romanian politicians, and withheld from me. And when

Portrait in an Unfaded Photograph

my moods were at their darkest, darker than the superb beer I would drink in quantity, I knew beyond doubt that Carmen Sylva had laughed at my letter, had turned away a fellow artist, and was prepared to let me starve or be sent to prison, all without even so much as lifting a ringed finger to help.

Across the Empire

In the summer of 1896 I was glancing through a newspaper, and was just about to put it aside when I came upon the announcement that the Emperor himself would be travelling to Romania on a state visit, during which he would be received and entertained at Peleş Castle. I thought that no doubt Carmen Sylva would recite a celebratory poem of her own composition, and Franz Josef and his Empress, the other Elisabeth, would consent to listen to an organ recital or similar from the Queen in the castle's lavish Music Room. There and then the plan leaped fully formed into my head. I would travel to Romania and use the opportunity now granted to put myself forward in person to Carmen Sylva. And I would take my little pistol as well.

Leaving Bohemia behind, the journey across the wide body of the Transleithian part of the Empire, across Hungary, was tedious and uneventful. In a daze I changed trains and waited on platforms in outlandish places. If anything, I was worried that the visit would be over before I could reach Sinaia. The train rattled through towns and cities, and across broad plains. Fields and rivers, hills and woods moved slowly past the carriage windows. It was hot, and I was continually mopping my face and drinking the bottled water that I quickly bought when we stopped at a station, frightened that my agitation of missing the train when it started again would raise suspicion, and lead to an unfortu-

A Flowering Wound

nate revelation, either from my own lips by an Imp of the Perverse, or through the methods of the Hungarian rural gendarmerie. Sometimes I was able to buy a cool bottle of some local dark beer, and bread and cheese, and sometimes fruit. The Empire moved on by, stretching out like a long afternoon, as I sat still gazing at it.

Eventually the train started to climb out of Transylvania, up towards the southern rampart of the Carpathian Mountains. The track became a single one, and lunged on through deep narrow valleys, following the road between overhanging trees. The effect was singularly attractive and restful. Often there was the sound of plunging water to be heard, and the shadows of the beech trees provided relief from the burning sun of the endless skies.

To my very pleasurable surprise, I experienced no difficulty in crossing the frontier into Romania. The train had been growing more crowded; whether or not half the population of Hungary was going to gawp at their Apostolic Majesties and the King and Queen of Romania, I did not know or care. Papers were examined perfunctorily; the Hungarian and Romanian border guards' German was execrable, and as I did not understand either of their languages myself, no-one seemed inclined to linger or attempt to ask too many questions. Much later, as it seemed, when the train steamed into Sinaia, I felt that I had achieved my main task. In reality, of course, it was about to begin.

The winding streets of the little town were festooned with the flags and arms of both nations, with bright pennants and posters of their royal majesties. There was imperial Franz Josef, king of this, that, and the other, prince, duke, and archduke, and plenty more besides. When I was at school we had had to learn all the interminable list of Habsburg titles, but I had made it my business to forget most of them. And there was his wife, the Empress Elisabeth, like her husband

Portrait in an Unfaded Photograph

growing well into middle age, like him still slim, but in contrast looking young. In the crowded streets as I strolled I overheard much talk of Elisabeth: that she would be at Franz Josef's side for as short a time as possible, and that she intended to spend most of her time looking at horses, talking to gypsies and listening to their wild music. Portraits of the King and Queen of Romania were also numerous. Carol was almost glaring out at his little and still new kingdom from his pictures, as if ready to jump out and immerse himself in it, while his Elisabeth—Carmen Sylva—stood stately and reserved, dreaming her worlds of fiction and folklore in the cool mountains of their summer retreat.

There were no spare hotel rooms to be found, but I was able to secure a tiny room—hardly more than a cupboard, really—in a house inhabited by Armenians. I had fallen in with the man of the house when he had heard me asking a passer-by who looked as if he lived in Sinaia about the possibility of finding accommodation during the days of the royal visit. I had decided to pose as a journalist, as indeed I had sometimes attempted to be during the times when business was quiet at the bank. In Prague I had imagined that Sinaia—and indeed, most of Romania—would be filled with journalists, correspondents, painters, photographers, and all sorts and varieties of those who follow in the wake of royalty, making their livings by them, or seeking to do so. My suppositions seemed to have been proven correct. It appeared that there were cameras on tripods set up everywhere on street corners and blossoming on every balcony, and almost every man in the street seemed to be carrying a notebook or reading one of the numerous illustrated books, magazines, and newspaper supplements produced for the occasion.

The Armenian showed me to my miniscule room, which I paid for in advance. I did not bother to unpack my small

A Flowering Wound

suitcase, although I did place a blank notebook and a packet of pens prominently on the little table under the window, and made sure that my host noticed them. In the crowded kitchen the woman of the house offered to prepare me an omelette, which I accepted gratefully. Declining the offer of something to drink after my coffee, I wandered out again into the sunset streets of Sinaia, determined to reconnoitre the town, and work out best how to approach Peleş Castle itself.

I had decided that I would assassinate Carmen Sylva in the grounds of her castle. I had concluded that there were sound practical reasons for this. Although the streets of the town would be crowded, and the procession bearing the four monarchs and various family members and politicians would of necessity have to proceed slowly, I had also counted on the sides of the roads being lined with soldiers and police, to say nothing of agents wearing civilian clothes blending in with the adoring crowds. For a moment I thought it possible that the Armenian who had taken me in might have done so because of my appearance or some suspicious behaviour on my part, and even now was summoning the authorities to arrest me on my return to my room. But no. I put the thought from my mind. I could not have survived those last few years and travelled the hundreds of miles I had just done, if I allowed myself to dwell on such pointless musings.

Consulting the special commemorative map that I had bought on my arrival, I followed the twisting streets as far as the gates of the royal estate. There were guards on the main gate, dressed in extravagant uniforms, but also armed with the most modern weapons. My little pistol might be suitable for felling an unarmed woman, but not one of these. There and then my resolve wavered again; but a moment later I knew that I had to finish what had started those years ago when the postcard of Peleş Castle

35

Portrait in an Unfaded Photograph

had so mysteriously appeared. But I did turn around and saunter away, as I did not want to draw attention to myself. I might be famous enough, and throughout the world, in just a matter of hours.

As dusk descended I followed the road as it ascended the steep slope. There were still a few large houses partly hidden behind walls and trees and deep in their large gardens. Then I had left the houses behind, and the road narrowed down to a wide track. Eventually the path flattened out, and, as I caught glimpses of a tall tower, surmounted by a steep, turreted roof, I realised that I had circled around behind the castle and its surrounding gardens. I could not see any sign of a wall or fence or ditch, although I was certain that there must be some sort of barrier between the royal domain and the rest of the world. I decided to come back the next day, in daylight. In any case tomorrow was the day that the Emperor was to meet the King.

I slept unexpectedly well, and on rising I made a few jottings in my notebook, so that anyone glancing at it would think that I was a bona fide writer. I checked my little pistol. After a cup of coffee, I left the house and walked the same way that I had done the previous evening. Even early in the morning the streets were becoming thronged with people, all dressed in their best clothes. I knew that I probably looked quite shabby by comparison; but in a few hours that would be the last thing for me or anyone to worry about.

There were definitely no walls bounding the royal estate where I had walked. Perhaps further along they were still under construction, but where I stood all there seemed to be was a wide and shallow ditch, which I crossed without the slightest difficulty. Suddenly I heard the rustling of branches and the low murmuring of voices. I crouched behind a tree, and held my breath while two soldiers walked past,

A Flowering Wound

following the ditch. So there were arrangements for guards at least, but they looked ludicrously ineffective. When the soldiers were out of sight and earshot I continued on into the woods, aiming towards the tower of the castle. At last the trees ended, and I found that I was at the edge of a lawn that ran down towards the rear of the castle. I sat down with my back against a tree, watching, listening, waiting.

As the morning progressed, and the shadows moved with the sun, I saw a group of children run across the lawn, shouting, to a terrace on the other side, followed by some adults. I remembered that the grounds were to be thrown open for the day of the visit. It seemed to me that destiny was handing me my opportunity like an embossed card on a silver tray. I checked that I still looked at least passably respectable, and certainly so for a mere newspaper and magazine scribbler. I held my notebook so that it could be seen. Then I wandered out of the protection of the trees, across the grass, and around to the front of the castle.

Beneath the main terrace, where the gardens began to fall away quite sharply, stood hundreds of spectators. The men were looking around them and shading their eyes from the sun, despite their hats, and the women I'm sure were gossiping and sometimes attempting to point with their furled parasols. Everyone seemed to be chattering and laughing, milling around and waiting with expectation for the royal couples and other distinguished guests. I walked up to the corner of the castle, where a group of soldiers was standing. I walked past them unchallenged. I looked around me and pretended to write in my notebook. I smiled and nodded at the soldiers, and some of them nodded back. They did not seem to harbour any suspicions whatsoever. It was all so different to Prague and Vienna!

Now the crowd grew hushed. Boots stamped on gravel as at barked commands soldiers came to attention. Cere-

Portrait in an Unfaded Photograph

monial swords flashed in the bright sunshine. And then I saw the objects of attention stroll out onto the terrace. First there were the minor royalty and the politicians, but I did not have eyes for them, only the Queen. I noticed a rank of photographers, in waiting behind their massive camera paraphernalia. One or two of them were readying their equipment for when the posing was to begin. Journalists scrawled on pieces of paper. I walked towards them, looking around me and still myself pretending to write, like a man with his day's portion of words to set down as he examined every element of the scene and its players. Now King Carol and Emperor Franz Josef strolled along, the very model of brotherly amity. They looked remarkably similar: one bearded, the other whiskered and moustachioed, both in military uniform and standing erect. Queen Elisabeth trailed demurely behind her husband. I looked for the Empress, but saw no sign of her. I assumed that the stories about her really preferring to visit stables and gypsies had been true.

By now I was within a few metres of the royal group. I seemed to be unnoticed. I reached inside my jacket for my pistol. I dropped my notebook, and the riffling and fluttering of the pages made a whirring sound in the breeze that caught the attention of the man standing nearest to me. He looked straight at me. I recognised him as Sturdza, the Romanian Prime Minister. Maybe I was to shoot him too. I might as well disrupt the proceedings as much as possible while I had the chance. I rushed forward and aimed at the Queen. She stopped and stood perfectly still. Her right hand came up to her throat, but she remained calm. I looked into her quiet eyes, her infinitely sad eyes. I pulled the trigger, but my arm jerked as the gun fired, and it was Franz Josef who fell to the ground. There were shouts and screams. King Carol bellowed something; Sturdza tottered

A Flowering Wound

towards me; soldiers started to break ranks and raise their weapons. Cameras went off, flashing and smoking. I looked at the Queen again. I think she started to hold out her arms to me, but then I turned and ran. The last thing I saw—and I did not believe it at the time—was King Carol tripping over his wife's quickly and deftly outstretched foot. Then I was gone.

It was lucky for me that confusion reigned, and that the arrangements to secure the castle and grounds had been so lax. But even as I ran and ran I could not stop thinking why it was that at the last possible moment, that when given the opportunity I had planned for, that when it was presented to me, I had failed. Just as I had failed to shoot myself in 1892, due to an intervention, I had failed to shoot again now. But where was the intervention? That is, unless it was Carmen Sylva's intervention, somehow . . . After all, it had been her face that had held my gaze as I fired . . .

Rumours and possibilities

As far as I could tell I reached the road with no pursuers. I threw the pistol away, and it sailed deep into the quiet depths of the woods behind me. I forced myself to stop and recover my breath as best I could. I straightened my clothes and smoothed down my hair. I walked back slowly down towards the town, as the clamour grew louder in front of me.

Back in crowded Sinaia I asked what was happening, posing as a disappointed traveller who had arrived too late to see the royalty assembled at the castle. Rumours abounded. Some said the Emperor had been killed, while some said he had merely been wounded. Others declared that Franz Josef had been miraculously saved, and that King Carol had ordered that a church be built on the spot where

Portrait in an Unfaded Photograph

the he had fallen, as in Vienna when Franz Josef had escaped assassination in 1853. One man in a group said that the two Elisabeths were at the Emperor's bedside, while his friend scornfully said that the Austrian Elisabeth was still looking at horses while the Romanian one was dictating fevered articles for sensational magazines in Paris, London, and New York. The last comment I heard as I boarded a train was that Carmen Sylva had ordered that Franz Josef's body be laid in state under the opened glass ceiling of the castle's Hall of Honour, because the Emperor had admired the modern ingenuity of the concept and the solid tradition of its appearance and execution.

Once on the train I felt completely tranquil and drained. It was as if my mind had evacuated my body, leaving it to do what it wanted. And what it wanted was to flow into the contours of the seat, to follow its shape, and just *be* there. To do nothing, think nothing. I drowsed in the warm sun, waking and sleeping in alternate moments. When my mind returned to my body, for the first time I became aware that my action was bound to have consequences. All I had ever thought about was to commit a specific act. I had given no consideration at all to what must inevitably follow.

As I dozed I also dreamt. What would happen now? Whether or not Franz Josef lived, Austria-Hungary would have to react. A price would have to be paid and honour satisfied. I imagined that the Empire would soon present Romania with an ultimatum that it could not possibly agree to. It would be yet more severe if it did turn out that I had killed the Emperor. And even if King Carol and his government did accept whatever demands Vienna pressed upon its much smaller neighbour, in my reverie I felt sure that the people of Romania would not stand for it. At the very least there would be an uprising. The government would fall and the monarchy overthrown with it. The Romanian army

A Flowering Wound

would be no match for the might of Austria-Hungary as it staged an invasion to "restore peace". It would not be long before the Habsburgs controlled the country. Whatever its outward form took, the Empire would make sure that Romania was in reality no more than a puppet state, perhaps ruled by one of the many spare Habsburg Archdukes who littered the Empire. Franz Josef would have achieved the ancient dream of complete control of the Danube and an outlet to the Black Sea.

And then another possibility drifted into my mind, in which the invasion was stopped in the mountains, and a counter-attack drove the Austro-Hungarian forces far back into Transylvania. The Romanian majority in most of Transylvania would rise and assist in their liberation. The other oppressed nationalities of Franz Josef's polyglot Empire would rise in revolt. Austria-Hungary would be torn apart like a loaf of fresh and warm bread, and hungrily devoured. And my own Bohemia . . . In Romania King Carol would preside over a different age-old dream: that of all Romanians being united in one state: Great Romania. I envisioned Russia acceding to the loss of Bessarabia in return for "compensation" in Austrian Galicia. All Middle Europe and the Balkans would be reshaped.

As the train chugged on across Transylvania, I slept again, and a third possibility manifested itself to me. Austria-Hungary's invasion would be repulsed; but the mountains with their steep and narrow passes, thick forests, and precipitous waterfalls would become the battleground, as the arid stony barrier of the Carpathians also prevented Romania from gaining absolute advantage. I dreamt that the high valleys and lakes filled with blood, which ran down and drowned both combatant countries, as their youth was poured into a crushing machine or crucible that would also draw in the surrounding nations. Years of warfare would ensue until

Portrait in an Unfaded Photograph

mutual exhaustion and destruction forced an unsatisfactory peace. The old certainties would vanish forever. Chaos would reign supreme.

I reached Prague, mind and body all but shattered. I snatched a newspaper from a vendor outside the station, throwing the few heller at his outstretched hand as I stumbled along the pavement. Once back in my room, with the door locked securely behind me, I tumbled into a chair and began to read the newspaper.

An unknown assailant had shot Emperor Franz Josef on his visit to Sinaia. The bullet had ricocheted off one of the Emperor's many medals and lodged itself harmlessly in the castle façade nearby. Franz Josef was knocked to the ground by the impact, spraining an ankle and cutting his hand. The would-be assassin had made good his escape in the pandemonium; King Carol and Prime Minister Sturdza being unable to catch him at the scene, and all subsequent attempts to apprehend him having failed. Naturally, the article reported, there had been mass arrests of suspected anarchists and other undesirables both in Romania and Austria-Hungary; King Ferdinand of Bulgaria and King Aleksandar of Serbia had also taken the opportunity to order certain arrests. In the meantime, interrogations and searches were proceeding apace. Another article said that Queen Elisabeth herself bandaged the Emperor's cuts with strips of cloth torn from her own voluminous sleeves, and had assisted him to his feet and helped conduct him to a comfortable couch within the castle.

I heard shouting in the street. Looking out of the window, I saw newspaper sellers hawking another special edition. The governments of Romania and Austria-Hungary were in frantic negotiation. This party or that called for an ultimatum or immediate declaration of war; while others urged moderation and the peaceful satisfaction of any grievances.

A Flowering Wound

I remembered my dreams, the way each was so real at the time, how they were each mutually exclusive; only one could ever come to pass and bring its world into painful birth. Whatever happened, however, Europe—if not the entire world—would change, I would have caused it. My actions and my actions alone caused it. Despite the reason behind what I had done: the fact that Carmen Sylva had rejected me, at that moment I knew that I could not blame her.

Over the next few days I stayed in my room nearly all of the time, not going to my desk at the bank, and not going outside until after dark. I sat in the dimmest corners of cafés and bars, reading newspapers by the ghostly flickering of gaslight or lamplight. The ultimatum to Romania demanded by the war-making parties did not seem to be going to materialise. It was as if a secret arrangement had been made behind the scenes, which had satisfied honour all around and saved face. I imagined the dark and rich wood-panelled halls and corridors of Peleş Castle filled with soberly-dressed and top-hatted statesmen, bemedalled military warlords, and the two stern-faced monarchs and their glittering consorts.

One evening, while pacing the streets near my room, I secured a copy of yet another special edition, rushed out so quickly that the newsprint was more damp even than usual. It contained the formal announcement that a treaty had been signed. King Carol was to abdicate in favour of the Crown Prince, his nephew Ferdinand. Austria-Hungary pronounced itself fully satisfied with that result; no doubt our Foreign Ministry was anticipating that Ferdinand would be easier to deal with than his uncle. At the back of my mind I entertained a lurking suspicion that everyone had underestimated Carmen Sylva, and, so too, now that she was all set to move into the foreground, Ferdinand's young and beautiful wife, the English-born Crown Princess Maria.

Portrait in an Unfaded Photograph

The next morning I decided that it was safe enough to resume my life in Prague. I returned to the bank, and made excuses about my longer than planned absence, saying I had been ill whilst staying in Pressburg, and so had remained there until fully recovered. The main topic of conversation was still the assassination attempt and the consequences flowing from it; I pleaded ignorance and feigned a lack of interest. This continued for the rest of the week. But everything changed on the following Monday.

Several letters were awaiting me when I arrived home late in the afternoon. They all looked routine, and I tossed them aside one by one until I came to the last one. It bore Romanian postage stamps franked with a Bucharest postmark. The handwriting on the envelope was flowing and extravagant, almost covering the entire remaining space on the front. I opened the envelope carefully, slitting it with a knife. The letter was written on Queen Elisabeth of Romania's personal notepaper.

My Dear Friend—

Yes, of course I know who and where you are, as indeed I knew all along, as soon as I saw you at Peleş. You have turned out to be a remarkable man; my initial enquiries being clearly in error, and so I was misinformed. But now I am glad about that. Everything is working out to our advantage, yours and mine. For the moment I must request you to keep absolutely secret the intelligence that I am going to give you. It will be common knowledge soon enough; but, my Dear Friend (and I feel that I am right to call you that), I wish to lay further plans that involve you, and so it is only right that I take you into my confidence, as I do now.

44

A Flowering Wound

You will no doubt have read the reports that my husband is giving up the Throne of Romania. He took up the responsibility and has discharged it; he is able to leave it. What you may not know is that I do not support even the concept of monarchy, and certainly not one for my beautiful adopted home that consists entirely of foreigners foisted upon the people without their consent. Ferdinand's son was born at Peleş, and so is the first true Romanian of our Dynasty; but time cannot wait for the second Carol. Dear Ferdinand does not want to be a king—he is much more happy amongst his plants and books than in the palace. He would be a good and dutiful king, but I have no wish to see him assume responsibility that he does not in his heart want, and which he will not discharge with any joy. I support Ferdinand in his desire to renounce the Throne, and Maria will do so too. Needless to say we are not breathing a word of this to my husband! When we have left the country, Ferdinand will, in his turn, abdicate and turn over his powers to a Regency Council. I will be called back to my beautiful Sinaia to play my part, but it will only be a matter of time before the monarchy is abolished and a republic proclaimed in its place.

No more will Romania have to rely on outsiders. Romania can and will stand up proud and great, and play its part in the development of Europe. My Very Dear Friend, you have helped this dream to start to become a breathing reality. My foolish actions (or inactions) when you first wrote to me may also show that some Higher Power is working out its purposes through us, you and I.

I ask you to send me a postcard of Hradčany Castle. It will reach me. This will be the signal to show that

Portrait in an Unfaded Photograph

my trust and faith in you has been justified, and rewarded with your forgiveness. I will arrange for you to receive a passport under a new name. When I am returned to Peleş, in time I will send for you to join us here; your safe conduct is guaranteed.

And now adieu—
Carmen Sylva

Out of the past

There is really very little more to write. Ex-King Carol returned to his family's castle in Germany, and ex-King Ferdinand and his family retired to England. I gave up banking for writing. Eventually I arrived back in Sinaia, to a Peleş Castle that was undergoing remodelling to Carmen Sylva's taste, the gift of the grateful citizens of the young Romanian republic. Sinaia became an artists' and writers' colony, presided over by its creator, Carmen Sylva. To start with, she encouraged me with judicious introductions and by graciously collaborating with me; I collaborated with the child prodigy Enescu, writing several operatic librettos for him to set to music. Many gifted writers, musicians and painters flocked to Sinaia under Carmen Sylva's enlightened reign of art and culture. And I started to create my own work. I wrote my *Walpurgisnacht* and *The Angel of the West Window* here in this very room; and, for as long as I am able, I will continue to write. I believe the name of Gustav Meyrink is not without those who appreciate it.

And now, fifteen years after the death of our bountiful patroness, new clouds are gathering. Ferdinand's son has started to call himself King Carol II and is acting like the exiled monarch he never was. Certain politicians in Romania are backing him, and a royal restoration seems not

A Flowering Wound

impossible. Carmen Sylva's power over kings and emperors was profound, but there is now no-one left with one quarter of her influence. I fear for my adopted Romania, my native Empire, and indeed all Europe. There is to be no miracle. Like a monstrous golem the aborted past rumbles ever closer, and I have no idea what to do.

The Golden Mile

He who binds to himself a joy
Does the winged life destroy;
But he who kisses the joy as it flies
Lives in Eternity's sun rise.

– William Blake

Every weekday morning at the same time Harry Wilsham would set out for work. He held a position as a junior accounts clerk in the main office of one of the vast new factories that had been built facing on to the Great West Road. When he had accepted the job Wilsham had been assured that there were "prospects" for the right sort of employees, but now there were times when the only attractive prospect seemed to be the one he could see from his desk rather than any advancement or fulfilment. The looming future seemed to be a solid wall instead of an opening door.

Although the Great West Road—a wide, almost completely straight motor boulevard—had only been constructed less than a decade earlier, the section where Wilsham's employers has established themselves was already well-known as the "Golden Mile". The company had invested heavily in its magnificent new headquarters and manufacturing plant, and regularly stated that it intended to expand significantly during the coming years. Wilsham

A Flowering Wound

liked to think that the palatial building in which he worked could be taken for a luxurious private residence. In common with many of the others lining the road on either side, it stood behind a beautifully maintained lawn punctuated by dazzling flowerbeds. A main driveway led straight to the main entrance, placed in the centre of the low, wide main block. Footpaths leading to other entrances and around to the factory blocks cut through the expanses of grass and skirted the masses of flowers. To Wilsham the overall effect of the building was of an ocean liner in dry dock, with its rows of windows and sleek horizontal lines running from end to end. The great length of the façade was interrupted only by a number of small staircase towers, each topped by a flagpole, and all complemented the soaring main tower—expertly placed off-centre—that drew the spectator's gaze ever upwards to where the company's name shone out against the white stucco during the day and pulsed with neon by night. And as if that had not been enough, the tower was capped by a gigantic three-dimensional version of the company's trademark symbol worked in glittering stainless steel. It caught the sun whenever it shone, and beams from hidden spotlights illuminated it during the hours of darkness. The neon lights and sculpture had rapidly entered motoring lore as prime landmarks for travellers entering or leaving London by that route.

When the weather permitted, Wilsham liked to walk all the way from the small terraced house in Acton where he still lived with his parents. It was not a great distance, and he liked exerting himself. As a child he had often accompanied his father on long walks on the western and south-western outskirts of London, sometimes wandering far afield to such places as Twickenham and Teddington, or Ealing and Perivale. The older man rarely walked there now, complaining that the fields and lanes he remembered

The Golden Mile

had been swallowed up by new housing estates, shopping parades, and wide arterial roads.

Once, when they had been to watch football in the new stadium at Wembley, his father had reminisced about the unfinished tower that had formerly stood on the site. The young Wilsham's imagination had been captivated and set aflame by the thought of what might have been: a metal titan higher than the Eiffel Tower punching into the sky above the North Circular Road. But the boy's dreams were brought down to earth; before he was born the project had been aborted and the gigantic fragment blown up and swept away.

Yet from that memorable day onwards intimations of tremendous possibilities to come never quite deserted him. As Wilsham grew up he watched London transform. Again and again, in plain sight, the immense entity changed into something else—and in a fresh form. Slowly, Wilsham became convinced that the new structures of concrete, brick, and glass together with the sweeping thoroughfares and sprawling estates meant other transformations too. Spending a day in the City and West End or taking a walk along one of the main roads near his house became an exercise in exploration; turning the corner into an unfamiliar street an adventure. He kept his thoughts to himself—he would be able to tell when and with whom it was right to share. Wilsham knew that whatever his parents' and friends' hopes and expectations were, a part of his own would surely be bound to the constant ebb and flow of possibility and opportunity embodied in what he saw as he looked around him each day—whether in the end never to be realised, or not as yet brought to birth from their creators' desires and diagrams. And still he knew this could not be all. Much seemed obscure, uncertain. There would be a day, as the way became clear or he apprehended it at last, when his

A Flowering Wound

awakening would be an embrace as well as an escape; a beginning as much as an attainment.

Each morning Wilsham would kiss his mother and leave the house, walking through the tangle of brick-built streets until he reached Turnham Park. It was only a few hundred yards from his part of Acton to Turnham Park, but it was a different world. The streets became wider and were lined with trees; the houses were much larger, sitting impassively alone or in pairs and surrounded by gardens and dewy lawns behind well-trimmed hedges and white-painted fences. When he reached The Green, Wilsham would decide whether to continue straight to the High Road and catch a bus the rest of the way, or wander on through the outer parts of the suburb until he emerged further down the main road in Gunnersbury, not far from where the Great West Road began. From there he could spy in the distance the slim, tapering white tower that rose high above the entrance to his place of work. On sunny mornings the device at its top shone and sparkled as if signalling to him.

But Wilsham no longer always paid attention to the far-off tower. Increasingly he felt closed-in, stifled. It was often too much of a struggle to recapture the old sense of impending adventure and the conviction that something novel could be awaiting him around every corner, if only he could perceive it. Every corner shop and every lamp-post in the little web of streets where he had lived for all his twenty-five years was familiar to him and gave out, on the surface at least, a sense of contentment and calm, even when money was short and employment precarious. The inhabitants of the district—people like him and his parents—were friendly and well-disposed towards Harry Wilsham. He went drinking and to the football with the same friends he had grown up with. But all of this was

The Golden Mile

on the wrong side of a wall—and one that seemed to be getting higher.

There was one more reason—the most important—why Wilsham wished that he could feel other than he so frequently did: his fiancée Winifred. She lived directly across the road and was considered an attractive girl, one who—to be honest—had the pick of any of the young men and need not have chosen Harry Wilsham. But she had. He knew he loved her, but so often he would glance at a newspaper or recall a cinema newsreel and think about all the uncertainty in the world. He often thought in vague terms about things he would like to do or try to discover, even as the words he wished to use to express clearly his agitated thoughts were not quite making themselves available to him. And so he kept them to himself. He felt there was too much he wanted to do and to find out, but didn't as yet even know what they were or would be; only that they were there and he would know one day. He knew all this was not really fair to Winifred—or to him.

The journeys to and from work—and particularly the walks in the early morning—were fast becoming the only times when Wilsham felt he could *think*; could be on his own with his thoughts and commitments and set them in front of the world around him and the people he spent his life with; could consider himself and dream of what it might still be possible to make of himself.

It was only lately that Wilsham had started to recognise that help might be presenting itself to him through the agency of a new "ally". When he did recognise it, the old dreams flooded back. The following Sunday he and Winifred had gone with friends on a picnic to Gladstone Park. They had all enjoyed themselves, as if there were nothing amiss for any of them. And yet at the same time Wilsham had successfully been able to detach himself and gaze out towards Wembley and imagine the view as if the great tower had been completed and still stood. No-one noticed that he had often been no more than a partial member of the party, and his purchase on the way home of the latest map of London and environs drew no comments.

The source of Wilsham's change was the third of the means available to him for travel to work: the Tube. It was the method he used least. This was mainly because he usually had to change trains and wait for the Piccadilly Line service; and his journey would still involve a lengthy walk from Osterley station. Recently, several stations along the line had been reconstructed or opened for the first time. When the new station buildings at Turnham Park were fully unveiled, what Wilsham had seen had woken within him a new dream of anticipation and release. Its strength had taken him by surprise: he had resigned himself to having lost such things for good. The tall, narrow brick tower of the rebuilt station was topped by a strange and twisted form or finial, its shimmering copper surfaces already turning green. The curving rods and planes combined to suggest what seemed like a skeletal bird about to fly free of the earth and swoop off into the sky and beyond. The finial was soon a great deal in his thoughts; he relished seeing it every morning and evening. And at Osterley the new station was dominated by a concrete structure like an obelisk, which seemed to symbolise both futurity and stability. Now there were mornings when Wilsham preferred to travel by Tube.

Dawn was breaking one clear and frosty morning in January. Wilsham closed the front door behind him, adjusting his hat and scarf and taking care not to slip on the icy front step. Thrusting his hands deep into the pockets of his overcoat, he looked up, as he always did, at Winifred's window. The net curtain parted for a moment and he saw her wave to him before letting it drop back again. He smiled and nodded. Winifred was secure in the knowledge that she would see him that evening, as on most evenings. They would talk about when they would be able to afford to marry, and consider the sort of district where they would like to set up home together. They would go over the figures again and again. To raise their spirits Winifred would describe the china and cutlery she wanted to buy for best, and the latest improved models of radio sets, so he could listen in to broadcasts of football matches and concerts of music from up "West". Wilsham would smile at the phrase, but not say anything: although the West End lay to the east of them, that might not always be so.

As usual it took Wilsham only a few minutes to cover the short distance to the boundary where Acton changed into Turnham Park. The districts did not so much flow into each other as collide. Even the paving slabs and lamp-posts were of different types on either side. The street changed its name, widening abruptly and becoming a "Way". The glass cupola on the roof of the great brick house on the corner blazed in the first light of the rising sun. In the frigid air his breath billowed and rose towards a sky of such a deep blue that for a moment he wanted to leap and fight his way up into it. He reached The Green, all covered with a layer of frost smooth as icing, and decided to walk directly across it so he could leave the trail of his footprints behind him. They would soon be obliterated by the sun as the long shadows retreated, but he would have made a mark, however brief. He didn't care about the shoes he'd laboriously polished the evening before, as on every evening when he took them off as soon as he got back from work.

The bare crowns of the trees around The Green were beginning to shine as the dawn light struck them. A train

A Flowering Wound

slid by on the railway embankment, scattering sparks. Wilsham looked up at the slender tower of the Tube station where, at the top, the bricks were beginning to glow a reddish-orange. The finial surmounting the tower shone with an inner radiance—the pale jade of spring buds and the first leaves of the hedges outside the houses lining the far side of The Green. The dawn had reached the red brick expanses of the vast cube of the ticket hall. Keeping the leaping, fluid form of the finial fixed in his mind, Wilsham turned away and walked on along Russell Avenue, heading towards a different tower—one he could not as yet see. He would spend the rest of the day in its shadow, not leaving it behind him until night had fallen once more.

When Wilsham left work the following Saturday the day seemed far gone even though it was only a little while past noon. The sky was low and grey; a steady breeze blew, but it was damp and mild. He had made no definite plans. He had turned down an invitation to watch Brentford F.C. play a match at home. The thought of a few pints before the game had appealed to him, and at first he almost decided to go. But as Wilsham watched his colleagues dart across the yawning gap of the Great West Road he was even more aware than ever that he now had the rest of the afternoon to himself, and no idea what he was going to do with it. Time stretched out all around him, as flat as Middlesex. As long as he was back on time for his dinner at Winifred's, the hours between now and then were entirely free.

He began to walk aimlessly along the Great West Road, following it in the direction of Osterley. As yet he couldn't see the Tube station with its tower and obelisk. On either side of the road were the offices and factories, car showrooms and warehouses that formed the Golden Mile of grand buildings of sheer white stucco or intricate brown brick, with their towers and gatehouses, staircases and driveways, their gaudy decoration and sculptured embellishments, the names of the companies and brands picked out in modernistic lettering and illuminated symbols. The buildings opened out in front of him as he walked, looking like stage scene façades against the lowering sky and rushing clouds. Wilsham walked steadily, as if along a corridor. Buildings approached, opened out and drew level with him, and then slipped away behind. And still the Great West Road ran on before him, rolling out like a concrete carpet longer than the store of hours that lay in wait for him.

The tall brick bulk of a church loomed up, the rounded end of the chancel and its steep roofs towering over the houses surrounding it. The church seemed to have turned its back on the main road and its ceaseless traffic. The road was now bordered by houses, raw and new. Gardens were patches of bare earth and broken bricks. He reached Osterley station and stopped for a moment, gazing at the massed brickwork and the pale obelisk stabbing up into the tumbling grey sky, cleanly etched against it. He sighed deeply and continued walking. Soon the station had fallen behind; still he walked. A light drizzle had been falling for a while when he stopped and tried to work out where he was. It was dusk. He was not far from Hounslow Heath; he knew where to find the bus stop from which to catch a Chiswick and Hammersmith bus. It would pass along the High Road close to Turnham Park station and home.

It was fully dark when Wilsham climbed down from the bus. The High Road bustled with activity and the pavements were rippling lakes of reflected yellow light. The Tube station was lit up from within, the soft glow radiating from the great windows and entrances. Its bulk rose into the night, outlined against the dull orange cloud scudding overhead. It reminded him of a giant radio set warming up and coming to life; the safe comforting glow of dials and valves and piercing smell of burning dust from inside keeping darkness at bay. The finial seemed to radiate light from within itself, although he did not know how this could really be. Perhaps there were built-in lamps or something. But poised on its tall brick column, as if ready to soar up through the low layer of cloud and gathering fog and into space, it rested, as if awaiting only the signal of release.

By the end of spring the arrangements for the wedding had been settled. But Wilsham's unvoiced anxieties for his and Winifred's future had not been calmed. He started to pay greater attention to articles on international politics in the newspapers and to cinema newsreels. All the talk was of Britain rearming; and the events on the Continent in March, when Germany had unilaterally remilitarised the Rhineland, seemed to him to indicate that great forces were preparing to draw a set of heavy curtains across the European—and possibly wider—stage.

On the day the wedding date had been finally fixed, Alf Wilsham took his son to the Royal Oak for a small celebration. To begin with he had merely hinted that now Harry was about to assume at last all the responsibilities of manhood and of providing for a wife and family there were very probably things he might want to know more about. Much to the relief of his father the younger man had gently let it be understood that he need harbour no concerns.

Going to the pub together developed into a weekly ritual. Wilsham was somewhat surprised and, at first, not a little embarrassed at the new attention his father was paying him. The two men had always got on extremely well when in each other's company at home, and that had been sufficient for them. Wilsham soon found his father's new approval—or, rather, augmented approval—of him to be enjoyable and

The Golden Mile

something he wished to ensure would continue after his marriage. The older Wilsham would buy the first round (and allow his son to treat him in return) and talk about his own young adulthood and entry into the real world of family life. He told Harry that even if he had seen the Great War coming—which in his view hardly anyone had—he was still glad that he had been married with a young son by the time war came and knew his duty to go and fight. "What if you had been killed?" Harry had asked. "Uncle Reg was. How would we have coped then? Or if you'd been gassed and not able to get your old job back?" Alf Wilsham put his empty glass down. "But I wasn't, was I," he said. "If we could tell the future we'd never get up in the morning. Anyway, you shouldn't? worry. There won't be another war. You've got a better job than I've got, and you're going to have a lovely wife. Win is a great girl. Both me and your mother have always thought so. Your future is made. Now, your round I think, Harry boy."

Wilsham had agreed to the suggestion, made by Winifred's widowed mother, that he move across the street to her house and set up home there. It would only be a temporary arrangement. Winifred was pleased, as it would mean that she would not have so many things to worry about, and they would be able to save a great deal more of their wages and put the money towards a nice new house further out from Acton. "Out past where you work, Harry," Winifred had said. "There are lots of nice new houses, nice and big, with big gardens and lots of fresh air. And you can get there so fast and comfortable on the Tube."

As summer advanced Wilsham walked to work through a Turnham Park transformed. Although he still left home at the same time—early, to allow plenty of time for his journey—the sun was already high in the sky. The heavy foliage

A Flowering Wound

of the trees, moving slightly in the warm and dusty breeze, was welcome as he strolled along the gently curving streets.

One morning he was up and about before dawn. It had been announced that the ledgers and files filling the office were to undergo a thorough audit, and Mr. Passington had intimated to him that a few hours of unpaid work outside of normal office hours would not go unnoticed—or, eventually, unrewarded. Preferring to start early rather than finish late, Wilsham had agreed to be ready at his desk much earlier than his usual time.

As he crossed The Green, leaving a trail of footprints in the dew, he looked up at the finial crowning the brick tower of the Tube station. The first full rays of the sun were iridescent on the highest point of the sinuous form. It occurred to him that the obelisk standing over Osterley station would also be catching the early sun, its white concrete bright against the paling silver sky. Now a feeling of expectancy welled up within him. It was like the way he felt when turning on the radio for a broadcast he had particularly been waiting for, or when the curtain rose on a film he and Winifred had been looking forward to, and she was gripping his hand tightly as the opening music swelled up into the vast darkened spaces of the cinema auditorium.

As more of the soaring finial caught the rising sun, it trembled and flickered as if it were about to launch away. All at once, to Wilsham it symbolised the step he was about to take. It was the way through and in to it: a gateway. And if he got on the Tube and travelled to Osterley, he could come out under the obelisk there, another gateway, and join the world. Wilsham walked through the entrance under the tower and bought his ticket. Soon the sleek train drew in.

As the train accelerated Wilsham remembered the long walk he had taken the previous winter, out along the Great West Road beyond Osterley. He thought of the view out of

The Golden Mile

the window by his desk: the broad, smooth, bright avenue, an artery leading away from the city which would be almost empty at this hour. If he were walking that way along it he would be casting his shadow where he could see it. He would have to wait for that: this morning he would be going towards the sun as he walked towards the crop of towers that had sprouted up on either side of the road. The Golden Mile would already be reverberating with all the activities of the new day.

The train clattered on, the carriage rocking gently from side to side. He remembered more of Winifred's plans for their new house, as yet unbought and unlocated. (Perhaps he was getting closer, even now.) "I like the name Shangri-La, don't you Harry? You know, like in that book. It'll be our nice place." Wilsham visualised the sort of house she meant. He shuddered at the thought of the half-timbered gable above the bay window at the front, identical with that of the house next to it. But he could not be clear why he should take against a house like that just now. Unless . . . Great West Road . . . The name represented for him the lure and joy of travelling . . . away . . . from . . . out of . . . over a frontier . . . into a new country . . . change . . . adventure . . . finding a place . . . sharing it with someone; the chance to find . . . to share himself. The swaying carriage was his life: comfortable and yet confined; mapped out and yet with no true certainty. There could always be a crash; something disastrous might occur at any time.

The train slid out of Boston Manor station. Osterley station was the next stop: his stop. He had embarked on this journey, entering through one gateway under its strange sign, and now another awaited him, just up ahead. It was approaching fast; in a couple more minutes he would pass under it and return to—well, everything as it had become.

A Flowering Wound

He stirred in his seat. Outside the window rooftops and trees were now fully bathed in the glare of the sun. As the train began to slow, he stood up and then sat down again. "Make up your mind, mate," a voice growled, before laughing. Wilsham blushed. Perhaps he should have walked after all, approached from the other side.

As the platform smeared itself along the window Wilsham knew what he wanted to do and where he was about to go. Even as he settled into his decision he was still not at all sure how he would reach his destination; but he knew that it need not be so very far away.

Falling Into Stone

Our name was my idea. The rest of it, all we did, was Josh's.

"We're living in hard times," Josh says. "Almost everyone's in trouble. But some aren't." He grins at me. He knows I'll go along with him—I always have done, ever since school. I can't help myself. "You and me, Luke," he says. "We'll get through all this. If you can't beat them, join them. We'll cause a bit of trouble of our own, make people think. But only those people who can take it. You know the types I mean. They've got enough already."

Josh has that way of drawing you in, making you go along with him, saying we're doing this together. Not anymore. Whenever I like I can leave him behind.

Josh and me, we couldn't be more different. I mean in how we ended up. We grew up on the same estate and were interested in the same subjects at school. We both really enjoyed the art class and were good students. We both drew and made models, mainly of real and imaginary buildings.

Somehow things changed, or maybe it was in me all along. Josh decided he wanted to be an architect—but all I wanted was to be with Josh. I knew it could never happen—he wasn't interested, or maybe never realised how I felt. Josh's parents supported him while mine didn't seem

A Flowering Wound

very bothered with what I wanted to do. Maybe I wasn't bright enough, although I'm not stupid. Anyway Josh went to university and got the qualifications. We lost touch, but I never forgot him.

Next time we meet I'm working on a restoration job on these flats as a semi-skilled hand and he's in a suit telling the foreman what to tell us to do. Friday evenings in the pub he tries to be one of the lads again and almost makes it, but not quite. There's something gets between him and us now. But he tries hard—he's genuine about it.

Josh asks me round to his place for a few drinks and to watch a film—a lads' night in, he says. He's got an apartment. He calls it an apartment, not a flat. It's in one of the new blocks near the river. These blocks look like they've got tin roofs which would come off with a gust of wind, and they're all frames with a bit of brick stuck on. Josh's place is nice inside. The rooms are all shiny wood and smooth plaster. They're small, but look bigger because they're just about empty. But the stuff Josh has must've cost him.

We drink this dark beer from the bottle. It tastes like smoky bacon crisps, and I almost fall off the sofa when Josh tells me the price. He's got the latest entertainment system and he streams a foreign film, but there are subtitles and I like it. There are these kids who break into rich people's houses when they're out and leave messages to scare the rich people. They don't do any harm or damage or anything but they want to scare the rich people.

There's a great view from his balcony but after the film and a few bottles of that beer I won't go anywhere near it. That makes Josh laugh, which I still like—but he doesn't go near the balcony either.

"It's a brilliant restoration job we're working on," he says. "It's a classic apartment block. One of those streamlined façades where the line of the windows and balconies make

Falling Into Stone

it resemble an ocean liner. Everything is smooth and sleek. Nothing is wasted or unnecessary. The effect depends on massing and volumes and placement—no decoration or anything that doesn't follow its function. Less is more, Luke. Those apartments give austerity a good name. You don't need anything outside of yourself. I'm going to try to get an apartment in that block. I know some of the people behind the contract and I'll have a chance if they put in a word for me. It's who you know, eh Luke?"

Josh goes on like that for a bit. I don't mind. He can talk well when it's something he knows and likes. I remember from school. I'm glad he's doing okay. Lots of people aren't. After a while he says his girlfriend's coming round later otherwise I could stay the night. I don't see where but the floor would've been fine. Josh says, "We'll do this again, soon, Luke, all right?" Somehow I get home no problem.

On Monday I'm at the site but I don't see Josh. His boss is there though. He says something to the foreman and calls us all together. "Bad news," he says. He looks like he's been crying. "Our client is bankrupt. He's pulled out of the job. It's up to his lawyers now. We probably won't get paid what we're owed. You might have to wait. I'm very sorry."

The foreman sends us home. "Sorry, lads," he says. "I'll do my best with the management so you get some money to be going on with, at least." We're all on our phones calling girlfriends and wives and parents to tell them, and friends and contacts looking for new work. I wonder where Josh is.

A few days later I'm at home when Josh calls. I haven't found another job. I don't remember giving Josh my number but I must have. He invites me round his place. "Might as well finish the last of this," he says, giving me a bottle of the weird beer. "I'm out of here." I look at him. He looks as smooth as ever, but there's something about his eyes. He grins. "Yes, Luke, I've lost my job too," he says. "I've been

A Flowering Wound

made redundant. The firm can't keep everyone on now the jobs we were doing for Mr. Bankrupt have packed in. I can't believe it—we never got the money up front." He looks around the room. It looks emptier. "I've got to sell all my stuff, everything that isn't being repossessed. I can't rent here anymore. Sarah's not coming round—ever again. Not now."

I say the usual things. I'm about to say less is more and all that, but don't. Josh grins again but it's a show. "We were going through a rough patch, to be honest," he says. "We would've split up anyway, sooner or later. It's just happened sooner. Now I really need to know who my friends are, Luke."

❦

I put in a word for Josh and he gets a room in the big old house I share. It's small but okay. He's sold or given away most of his stuff. "It hadn't been paid for anyway," he says. "They're welcome to it." Josh is on his laptop all the time but none of his old mates from university or the firms he knows get him anything. I get a bit of casual stuff, enough to pay the rent and buy a few tins of beer at the weekend. Nothing's much different from before—there's just less of it. Josh gets more and more angry. I can tell. "This isn't where I'd planned to move to," he says. Mainly he keeps it bottled-up inside, but I can tell. One night he knocks on my door and we go to his room for a beer. Tins of lager, but they're okay. His room is as bare as his old apartment was, but there's no balcony and the view from the window isn't as nice.

"You remember that film we watched when you came round to my last place?" Josh asks. "I've been doing a bit of thinking. There are lots of houses, big, posh houses, empty some if not all of the time. And you and me, we're in a dump like this. They say we're in hard times, but not everyone is. Luke, you and me, we can make it a bit softer for ourselves. And have a bit of fun, harmless fun. Are you up for it? Just until things get better."

I still don't know why I say it. I have no idea where it came from. "You mean like austerity outlaws?" I say. "You and me—we'll be austerity outlaws?"

Josh grins and laughs. It's the first time for a while. I'm happy about that. "You're a genius, Luke!" he says. He throws me another can of beer. "Let's drink to us—the Austerity Outlaws!"

Josh makes up a logo we can draw on pieces of paper or card and leave behind us. I tell him I recognise the A for Austerity but not the other letter. He says it's still an O, but from the Greek alphabet. The whole thing can mean from the beginning to the end. I don't really get that, but it's a nice logo, easy to remember and draw. I practice it a few times to get it right. It takes me back to art class—the best part of being at school.

It's fun being an Austerity Outlaw. Josh knows about a lot of very nice places that are empty or where the people are away. I suppose it's through his old contacts. We're careful. There have to be no alarms or security, but sometimes they're so easy to dodge or fix it's like there's no security at all. Josh sorted out some electrics once or twice—I don't know where he learned to do that. If we do have a problem we run like hell. We never get caught, not me and Josh.

So we go into these houses. We move the furniture around, leave pictures at an angle, that sort of thing—harmless but scary to come home to. Sometimes we take food or something to drink, but we don't steal anything. We don't damage anything either. Josh says austerity should be creative, not destructive. He says everyone else can do the

A Flowering Wound

destroying. Sometimes we work hard and move furniture and valuable objects into another room to make it look like there's been a robbery. He likes it when we've made a room bare. He says that's how it was meant to be—just space to live in, which should be enough. We leave our message and go. "Let them find out how less really is more," Josh says.

Josh looks in his book a lot. It's a sort of guidebook to modern buildings and houses. There are little photos of each one, and plans. He says it's the only book he's got left. "These are some of the finest modern houses in the country," he says. "I studied them at university. The apartment block we were restoring is in here. Actually those sorts of places aren't very modern by age. Most of them were built between the two World Wars. It was a classic era." He closes the book and turns to me. "You know, Luke, back then it was like now. No—probably even worse, actually. The Great Depression. There was high unemployment, cutbacks, poverty. They taught people to be suspicious, to hate. If you had money you were fine. If not, you weren't. You could do anything if you had the money. Keep in with the right people, live like a king. Money always talks. And if you lost it, you were lost, too."

I like it when Josh talks that way, even about bad things. I can listen to him. I don't always know what he's on about, but I can tune in and out and feel different for a while afterwards. "Your life, Luke, you fell off the scaffolding," he says. "You dropped, fell into liquid concrete, went down and down and ended up buried alive with all the others. It would've been a better end to hit something solid. Luke, neither is going to happen to me." Then he says quickly, "Or us, right?"

We get some warm days and Josh looks in his book. There are quite a few of these big classic modern houses in suburbs around the city or just outside. Josh says some of

Falling Into Stone

the owners have lost their money or are cutting back. Their places will be empty or closed-up or both—nice for us.

We hitch our way out to one of these houses. It's white and low and only just shows above the trees. The garden's gone wild and hedges and trees grow up all around it, in front of the windows and doors. The windows are huge, and are covered by metal grills or heavy plastic panels. The house is empty. We get in easily enough. It looks as if it's been empty for months.

When we're inside Josh gets out his book and we have a tour. This place is completely bare, but Josh says it was supposed to be all austere and minimalist anyway. "Less is more," he keeps on saying. He says there was hardly any furniture and all the cupboards and things were built into the walls. As far as I can tell you have to be very rich to afford to have so few things. Josh says he wishes we could see the rooms by full daylight as that's the best way. "It's the human scale." Then he says, over and over, "It's simply beautiful."

I feel something too. Maybe not like Josh, but I'm not him. There's lots of space, and the distances between the walls feel right, somehow. How they should be. The light comes in where it should and falls where it needs to. Everything seems to fit together. I think I could get used to living in a house like this. Josh talks about the workmanship, the craftsmanship, the quality of the materials, their cost. The walls are finished perfectly—Josh says most of them are concrete. But they don't look it—they seem too smooth, like fabric stretched out tightly. I push the palm of my hand against a wall, but it doesn't bend inwards like it looks as if it should. It's solid—firm and doesn't give. The floors are stone—travertine and marble, Josh says.

There's only the one storey, but it's not just a big posh bungalow. There are steps and ramps to the different levels in other parts of the house. There's also a spiral staircase

A Flowering Wound

leading to the roof, but we don't try to go up there and onto it in case anyone spots us. One room is a huge curved window all on one side, but it's covered by the thick plastic panels so the light is dim and distorted, like wearing smeared sunglasses indoors. Josh goes to the wall opposite the curving window. "This is really special," he says. "The wall's panelled with British marble, really rare. Look at the colours and patterns, Luke, the flecks of silver and gold. It's like they're floating above the colours but below the surface. It's cool to the touch, even in this weather." I have a look too. I'm floating above crumpled mountains and rivers are veins in the marble. The surface is still polished and smooth as glass. I could slip over and fall in. Josh laughs when I tell him. "I'll rescue you," Josh says.

His voice trails off and he turns to me and smiles. He's let his hair grow and he brushes a strand away from his face. I keep my hair as short as ever. Before I know it I begin to stretch my arm out, but Josh grabs it like we're going to shake hands and we do. No more than that, though. Josh never hugs. We go back to the big main room. It's all shadowy but we settle down in a corner and unpack the stuff we've brought for the night.

In the morning we leave our AO message. I have to remind Josh before we move on. He doesn't seem bothered if anyone's going to know whether we've been here or not.

⁂

We do this for a while. Then one time Josh asks me if I remember the house. When he shows it to me in his book I do for sure. "It's been bought by our old boss," he says. "Well, maybe he wasn't exactly that, but he's the man who declared bankruptcy and made us lose our jobs. How could he afford to buy a house like that now?"

Falling Into Stone

"He's on the way up," I say. "Money talks."

I ask Josh how he found out. "On my phone," he says. "It's easy. I had to check these sorts of records a lot when I was in the office." Then he gets out this phone and does a search. He shows me. I didn't know Josh still has his phone—it's one of the latest ones, very expensive. We're supposed to be getting rid of all our extra things. We can't carry stuff about when we're the Austerity Outlaws. Josh doesn't seem to notice how I feel.

He starts getting all angry again thinking about the house and its new owner. "He's got the money," Josh says. "Somehow he has. Or the right people reckon he's got it. Listen, Luke, we've got to go back there." He smiles, but it's a different type this time. Not one I like.

The grass is cut and some of the hedges trimmed back. The grills and panels on the windows have gone. There was a wire fence and notices about guards and a patrol with dogs but we didn't see anything.

There's no problem getting in again. These people haven't got a clue. We walk around the house. It's a different place with the light coming in. It's still empty but there's lots of builders' stuff piled in one room. We can see there's a layer of dust over everything, even on the walls. But the house seems sound.

Josh walks around and looks at everything, touching and sizing-up like he's buying it himself with his own money. He doesn't care how dirty he gets. I sit down and watch. Josh runs his hands over the walls and kneels down to touch the floors. He opens and closes doors and cupboards, stroking the wood like he's in love with it.

Seeing that doesn't make me feel good.

But what does is the way the sunlight comes in at angles. I can see it because of the dust. The light looks solid. The rooms breathe the light in, and the walls and floors suck

A Flowering Wound

it in like they're thirsty. They let me do that too. Shadows are waiting their turn.

"Everything is so right about this place," Josh says. "You see that, Luke?" He looks around, scanning the walls. "I should be on the way to getting somewhere like this, if it wasn't for the firm not getting its money."

I tell him I know what he's saying about the house. I mean it. Josh laughs. "Maybe you should've trained as an architect with me," he says. He sits down next to me. "You have the feel for places like this, I can tell from before." Josh is close. There's something different about him. If we'd had a few drinks I reckon I might say something. Man to man, good mates.

Josh goes quiet. I can tell when he's thinking, when something's getting to him. After a while he gets up and walks over to some sliding doors hiding some shelves. Josh says the wood is solid beech and the fittings are unique, designed only for this house. "I don't know why these doors weren't taken out for safekeeping," he says. "They should've stored all the ironmongery, too." Then he pulls a knife out of his pocket, one of the ones you slide open to cut plastic and boxes, and gouges our AO sign, big, into each door. He grunts with the effort. I jump up.

"Don't say anything, Luke," Josh says in this odd voice. We had a teacher spoke like that when he couldn't explain something properly so you couldn't quite get what he was on about. He scratches all the fittings as well. He moves so he's standing against the light. Josh is a shadow walking out of the sun, but solid, like a statue. Then he comes back over to where I'm still standing.

"You said we don't damage places," I say.

"The Austerity Outlaws don't damage places," he repeats, imitating my voice in a stupid way. "Luke, I haven't started."

I tell him no, but he pushes me away. "You really do appreciate this house, don't you, Luke? Modernist masterpieces like this? You could've made the effort, made a proper career for yourself, maybe a bit of money, one day you could have owned one. You might've had better luck than me. I might've been working for you by now! Do you want to borrow my book?" He pulls it out of his pocket and rips out some pages. He holds them out to me then takes them back again. Josh has this big shiny lighter, old fashioned. Something else he shouldn't have. He sets fire to the book and drops it on the floor. He pushes me away when I try to kick the fire out. It doesn't catch anyway, but the book's damaged and there's ash and bits of torn paper on the floor. Josh rubs it across the tiles with his foot, smearing it there.

"The Austerity Outlaws have had enough," Josh shouts. "I've lost my job, my place to live. All I've got is a crappy room in a crappy house and no-one wants to know me anymore." I want to tell him that he couldn't say that, and I do still want to know him. But we had a deal. The AO had a deal together. And we're supposed to be best friends.

"Austerity Outlaws is a laugh but this time I'm not laughing," Josh says. "Not in this house. That bastard doesn't deserve it. He's not going to have it. I'm really going to leave my mark. I'm not being buried alive like you. If I'm falling it's going to be onto a floor made of marble. I'll leave my mark all right." Josh goes into the room where all the builders' stuff is and comes out with a masonry hammer. He runs over to one of the walls and smashes the hammer against it two or three times. Plaster falls off and big cracks show. I'm standing some way away but in the room it's like explosions going off next to my head. My head's ringing like someone shouted right into my ear. I run towards Josh, but trip on a step where the room's level changes. I fall over, hitting the floor and scraping skin off my hands.

I can't believe it but Josh starts to laugh. I don't know what's got into him. He lets the hammer go so it drops on

A Flowering Wound

the floor, and the heavy thud of it hitting goes right through me. I put my hands to my head and there's blood where I scraped them. My hands are sticky and covered with bits of grit and plaster and tiny sharp bits from where Josh dropped the hammer on the floor. And there's some of my blood on the floor but it soaks in and disappears even as I look at it.

"Look what you've done," I shout at Josh. I hold my hands out. Maybe I hope he would hold them, take me to where we left our rucksacks so he would get out one of our bottles of water and wash my hands and clean ourselves up. Josh picks up the hammer. "Less is more," he says. "He's going to have less." He looks at my hands. "Why don't you rub them on the walls? Make yourself useful, Luke. He wants blood, he can have it."

Not for the first time since I've known Josh I want to cry. But I can't show him.

Josh kneels down, smashing the hammer down on the floor. "Less—is—more!" he shouts, as it hits the floor, cracking the stone. I thought he loved that stone. He shouts each word as he brings the hammer down, smash, crash. He does it again and again. I go and lean against the wall. I rub my eyes and it's painful but now it looks like they're hurt and not that I'm trying not to cry. There's a bit of my blood on the wall but it soaks in like it was never there. I lick my hands, and taste the blood and bits of plaster and tiny chips of marble.

"Luke!" Josh shouts from another room and I go to find him. I'm back to obeying him. He's in the room with the curving window. He's standing by the wall made from polished marble. My head starts to ring with echoes. For a moment I have the feeling of falling sideways, slipping into it, like before. Josh is covered in sweat, glinting on his skin in the sunlight filling up the room. He's gripping the hammer and there are cracks and gouges in the marble.

Falling Into Stone

There's blood on his forehead. He wipes it off with his free hand and looks around. Josh is about to wipe his hand on his shirt when he grins, the horrible grin, not the grin he uses for me, and rubs his hand against the marble. His blood stays there like someone's flicked red paint.

"What?" I shout. Josh just wants to make me see the damage he's doing. We had a deal—the Austerity Outlaws, no damage—but he's ruining it. He strikes the wall again with the hammer, sending more slivers of marble flying. Some of them cut him as I watch. I stand away so they can't cut me. Now he's trying to hammer our AO design into the marble. He's not getting very far, even though he's really damaging the wall. Josh drops the hammer and gets out his knife and starts scratching it against the polished stone.

"Look!" He screams as he tries to carve the logo. The knife slips all over the place. "I'm having it! This is going to be my house now!" I rush over to him to grab the knife but he swings it at me and I only just dodge out of the way. "You said no damage!" I shout, trying to make him listen to me. "We agreed, together. Not this!"

"All deals are off!" Josh shouts back. He stumbles into a slanting block of yellow light that was hiding in the room all the time. Now I see it, sliding in through the window, all the way down from the sun. It's a door opening. Josh goes in as if there's a new room and comes out again like from behind a curtain. He still looks like Josh but I don't know how much he is.

Then dust and bits of marble and concrete and chippings start rising up like fog and hiding the light. Everything swirls around in a sort of dirty blizzard. I hear hammers and engines and concrete pouring and blurry voices and laughing. I collide with Josh and try to pull him out of the room but he pushes me away and I slip over and I can't tell where to get out, then the marble wall is there to meet me.

A Flowering Wound

I start coughing and fall over again as I twist backwards. I know I'm shouting Josh's name but it's become a separate thing and anyway he can't hear me and I can't see him anymore. I never felt the wall, but the dust and fog follows me wherever I am. I roll down a step, cutting my hands and arms. The dust and fog follows me. I crawl around in the stony hard shadows and see my blood smearing on the floor. This time it stays there. "I'm out, I'm out!" I keep shouting. But marble is all there is to push against—its patterns of veins and forms.

Then I'm sitting in the sunshine with my back against a wall. It's clean and white, warm from the sun.

Sometime later I think about looking for Josh so we can get away together. I hear a noise, and he's coming out of the house. He looks a mess.

"Josh!" I shout. "Josh!" I try talking to him, all gently, like I've always really wanted to. "Josh," I whisper. He must be able to hear me—he turns his head. There's a beginning. But he stands there and doesn't say anything. I get closer, touch his hair and push it back a little. I lean in and gently brush away a splinter of marble from his cheek. Then I look into his eyes. All I see is me and the gleaming empty light. The light could be draining out of his eyes or already be outside wrapping us up. But inside it's completely bare. Behind Josh's eyes there's nothing left to value—everything's gone. They're as smooth and shiny and solid as the polished marble wall. The flecks in the marble are those in his eyes, too—just the same, embedded where there can be no depth. And now there's no help, nothing at all.

Ziegler Against the World

Gerold Ziegler had lied to his wife. As he had comforted her he told her he had forgotten what had happened in the dream, but that simply was not true. He stood in the little kitchen making the coffee. Ziegler could still hear Lotte's scream of shock and terror, no doubt caused by his own screaming. He shivered as he remembered how the dream had ended: he could not possibly have discussed it with Lotte. She would only want him to seek help, and he was sure that would only make things worse. He was convinced that the dreams would, in any case, come to an end when the reason for their haunting and possession of him also came to an end. He had accustomed himself to thinking of the nightmares as visitations that would leave him alone one day—he just wasn't sure when that day would be. It was all beyond his control: something to bring resolution would happen, one of these days. In the meantime Ziegler was left with the feeling that there was a balance waiting to be restored—in the depths.

The latest dream had been much the same as the others. He had been queuing in the post office to buy postage stamps, and was sharing in the bemused indignation of the others standing in line. Someone had pointed out the notice stating the latest postal charges, and the fact that at the new rate it now cost two million marks to post a letter to the other side of the city.

A Flowering Wound

"All that to get from Weissensee to Charlottenburg!" a woman said in disgust. "In the past I would have expected to sail in luxury around the world ten, fifty, times over if I paid that!"

"Yes, they must sort out this inflation, and soon," a man joined in loudly. "Two million marks! Why, before, one could have bought an entire estate in Pomerania or East Prussia for that!"

Ziegler noted that his neighbour had not said what the "before" he referred to was. But of course he didn't have to say: everyone knew. Not one of them in the queue would have wanted him to say. It was before the War—before August 1914, and certainly before November 1918 when the armies had trudged back to a different country from the one they'd left and which they'd been told they were fighting for. Germany was supposed to be their homeland, but their homeland was unrecognisable. The soldiers had been told that they returned undefeated: in which case, why had they not won? They asked why had the nation signed a dictated peace and been left to pay the reparations? That was where the real money had gone.

He bought his stamps. As he walked out into the street he thought that at least they weren't the overprinted ones. Whenever he had been given any, he'd felt it was adding insult to injury. Higher values—ever more fantastic ones—simply imposed on lower values, as if that would blot them out and hide what was happening to their money. He looked at the tiny row of zeros on his stamps—then it happened.

The zeros suddenly expanded like balloons being inflated. In an instant Ziegler was looking at a row of gaping mouths, open in soundless shrieks as they floated free from the stamps. He looked around him. People were walking to and fro along the pavement, not noticing or paying any attention to what was happening right in front of their eyes. The mouths' red lips drew back as rows of sharp teeth, white, glittering, slid into place. The open mouths circled around Gerold before lining themselves up behind him. A tram clattered past. He began to run.

Abruptly he was at his desk at the office, opening the battered tin box in which he kept the petty cash and postage stamps. There were no longer any coins, just a wad of worn banknotes and several sheets of stamps, folded to fit them into the box. The sheets wafted out of the box as he watched. They opened themselves out, and the stamps began to separate along their rouletted edges. The points became sharp teeth which raked his face. The stamps fluttered free, swirling around him like snowflakes. He shouted for help and tried to protect himself, but the stamps' razor edges sliced into his hands. Herr Fuchs looked up and smiled absently; no-one in the office noticed anything out of the ordinary. The zeros on the stamps opened up and began to scream and bite. Blood flowed down Ziegler's arms and soaked into his jacket. He jumped up from his chair, fighting off the shrieking paper, as he awoke to Lotte's scream and his own relief.

Ziegler returned to the kitchen after leaving a cup of coffee on the little cabinet at Lotte's side of the bed. He sat at the table and pulled apart one of yesterday's rolls and began to eat his breakfast. He was relieved that one part of his dream—so far as he knew—hadn't reoccurred. Or perhaps he had dreamed it again and it had been erased from his memory. But either way he couldn't tell Lotte. He was sure that would make her want to leave. The circular mouths full of shining teeth were bad enough; it was worse when he dreamed they were in the faces of real people. And it was worst of all when he dreamed of Lotte—and it was not her smiling and enticing mouth, but row upon row of pointed teeth, that stretched out to chew and swallow him.

A Flowering Wound

❧

Ziegler arrived at his desk almost an hour early. He intended to devote all that time to the task he had set himself. He worked as a reader and editor for one of Berlin's many book publishers; the firm published popular editions of all sorts of fiction, poetry, and drama, from the established classics to new and experimental authors. Ziegler imagined that one day he would submit a collection of stories or a play, and have them accepted—but he still had to write something of his own. Until then he contented himself with working at a translation. His employers published a line of German editions of foreign-language novels, and he was hopeful that his translation could be included.

The company naturally expected its employees, while on the premises, to put in a full day's work for their pay. But there was never any objection to anyone working on projects of their own outside office hours. Ziegler often took advantage of this. Besides, staying longer at the office in winter saved some of the cost of heating the apartment.

Lotte would often go to her mother's where the two women would prepare a late evening meal. Gerold would remain at the office for a few hours, after which he would collect Lotte from her mother's on the way home and also eat his share of the meal. He always ensured that he gave Lotte a few marks to pass on to her mother to help cover the ever-increasing costs. He also tried his best to make sure that his wife had enough so she could occasionally go out with her friends for coffee and cake, or with him to a café. In turn she liked him to be able to join his friends or colleagues for a glass of beer. The fact that what was once a few marks had turned into many million merely added a touch of the utterly surreal to their daily struggle to keep alive the modest lifestyle to which they had become accustomed—as well as their dignity.

Ziegler Against the World

Ziegler unlocked the drawer and carefully took out his copy of *Là-Bas* by Joris-Karl Huysmans. He had first read the novel, in the original French, while he was a very young soldier serving on the Western Front. His unit had cleared a small village. Its defenders had retreated or been killed in the fighting. Later he heard there had been some bayoneting as well, after the fighting had ended—but he had learned that all sides occasionally indulged in that. Assigned to burial detail, Ziegler helped load bodies onto stretchers and carry them to the cemetery next to the shattered church.

"Earth's so churned up we won't need to dig!" the soldier holding the other end of the stretcher muttered. "That's less work for us, laddie."

"What if there's an unexploded shell down there?"

He laughed. "Well, maybe we'll just get to where this one here's already gone and where we're all going, only just that little bit quicker."

"I want to get home again."

"Sure you do. Back to Berlin, isn't it? To the Capital City of the Reich? And what makes you think it'll be worth it?"

They were ordered to help dig a large communal grave. After a brief rest, they started to lay out the bodies of the dead French soldiers at the edge of the pit. Ziegler could tell that the bodies had been thoroughly searched: pockets had been turned inside out and choice items "lost". Sometimes boots and other useful equipment had also been taken. He began to drag one body closer to the pit when a small hardbound book fell onto the damp grass. He stooped and quickly picked it up, slipping it straight into his pocket without stopping what he was doing. Ziegler guessed that he and the dead soldier must have been about the same age. There seemed to be no trace of death on him; the young man could so easily have been sleeping. Ziegler stumbled and the corpse's mouth dropped open, revealing clean white

A Flowering Wound

teeth marred only by a large gap in the middle of the upper row. Just in time Ziegler stopped himself from glancing about for the missing tooth. He shivered and tipped the body into the grave with as much care as he could muster. For a moment the soldier's hand seemed to move, as if groping for something it should have been holding; the man's arm moved slightly, uncertainly, as if he were trying to wake himself up and rise out of a reverie. Ziegler batted the hand back, and there was a faint thud as it fell onto the body. If the soldier hadn't really been dead, he certainly was now, Ziegler thought. He went to drag the next body over to the hole.

Later, a weak counterattack was repulsed and they started to dig themselves in to their new positions. Corporal Metzger ordered his unit to make the church's relatively undamaged sacristy habitable. By nightfall Ziegler was exhausted, his body aching all over, his mind numb. But as he swallowed his soup and bread he could feel the book in his pocket. Its weight and bulk were negligible, but he knew it was there, an unexpected visitor that had already made itself at home and was biding its time. He didn't want to give anyone the chance to take the book away from him. And from then on when odd moments presented themselves he read his new possession, fingering its pale silk binding and turning the smooth and fragile pages slowly and with great care.

At first Ziegler did not know what to make of the book. It was called *Là-Bas* and seemed to be a novel; but he couldn't always be sure. The title—simple and direct as it was—nevertheless intrigued him. Deep down, deep below: he imagined gaudy medieval hells, but alive and at large in a world recognisable and real to him. It was the world he shared with everything he knew, which included everywhere and everyone dear to him. Nothing was beyond the

Ziegler Against the World

possibility of being an intrusion from flourishing survivals for which "deep below" could be their only origin—or destination. He thought of the pit full of dead French soldiers, and the ones packed with dead Germans. *Down there.*

The book's beautiful and delicate covers masked a story that perplexed him. It whispered new words to his mind as it insinuated itself into him, beneath his daily routines and duties. Deeper than he could hear the story spoke secrets meant only for him. Great ceremonies were constantly being performed; he would soon have the opportunity to take his place and join in, when the time was right.

Ziegler could read French well, and wished he could have talked with the book's original owner. Sometimes after waking up he was not quite certain whether or not he did. He didn't know if the dead man spoke German, but if not that presented no barrier. And if Ziegler's French was not good enough they surely expressed themselves in the veiled language out of the book. Sometimes he couldn't help thinking that his acquisition of the book had interrupted something, and that he had gained it under false pretences, and was really no more than a thief. All that through no fault of his own; all that despite the book having simply, and almost literally, fallen into his hands. He hadn't asked for it; he had saved it. And then, as he drowsed preparing for another discussion with the dead man, he knew that the new arrangement—clear and absolute—would again be confirmed.

On leave and at home in his parents' apartment just off Prenzlauer Allee Ziegler had time to read *Là-Bas* through from beginning to end, and closely, as he lay in bed in the still and solemn air of his high chilly room overlooking the second courtyard back from the street. On his arrival in Berlin he had wasted no time. He had left the station and visited a bookshop, buying a German translation of

A Flowering Wound

the novel, which he started to read as he waited for a tram. As well as re-reading the original text, he spent much time comparing it with the German text. What he found—and what was absent—dismayed him. A furtive sadness began to grow inside him, which he concealed as best he could. To his parents Gerold so often seemed to be missing, even though he was living with them in the apartment. Every day they saw him, sitting still or moving about, but their bewilderment would not leave them. Nevertheless they remained proud that their son was doing his duty for his country, even as he kept himself to himself and hardly wished to talk. Mother and father deprived themselves to give Gerold more of the gritty bread, *ersatz* coffee, and turnips that were sometimes all that was readily available to buy in the shops.

As Ziegler got ready to return to his unit his melancholy increased—not because of the reports from the Front or his having to go and take up his duties there again, but because of the responsibility he now knew he had been given. He started on his own translation of *Là-Bas*, but knew he wouldn't be able to finish it and make it as it should be until the war was ended and he was back home in Berlin once more, and for good.

❧

After demobilisation Ziegler had been fortunate in finding a job. He had been even more fortunate in keeping it. His marriage to Lotte brought him almost as much anxiety as happiness: there was now another person with claims on him, and any change in his situation would do more than affect only him. And Ziegler worked on his translation whenever he could find the time. He had tried to explain to Lotte—cautiously—something of his fascination with

Là-Bas, and she raised no objection to his spending time with a French novel that he could otherwise have spent with her. She was happy to know that he wasn't wasting his rare spare marks in one of the cafés near his workplace or in the neighbourhood bar at the corner. Lotte was proud of her husband for being able to continue earning a wage—barely adequate though it was—and for having a serious literary goal, no matter how unlikely it often seemed to her that it could ever be fulfilled.

As the value of money plummeted Ziegler became one of millions of paper billionaires who were no better off than they had been before. The young couple consoled themselves that at least they had no savings to be wiped out. Ziegler went to work as usual and worked on his translation when he could. Lotte asked to be involved, and Gerold let her make a fair typed copy of each day's work. He constantly revised and amended his translation, so that Lotte lost all sense of reading a sustained and coherent story. She encountered *Là-Bas* anew each day and built up a patchy series of shorter and longer fragments. She could not discern any over-arching shape or design. Gerold never made it clear how they joined up with each other—or if they ever really would. Nevertheless, the pile of paper grew thicker.

❧

One of Ziegler's duties at work was to unpack the frequently bulky parcels containing manuscripts and proofs that the company received each day. The proprietor would sometimes pause at Ziegler's desk as he pulled the wrappings off yet another handwritten manuscript. Although Dr. Ritter insisted all submissions be logged, he did not expect handwritten ones to be appraised, and would himself hurl them into Ziegler's wastepaper basket, unless he was told

A Flowering Wound

in time that return postage had been included or the paper was suitable for use as scrap.

As the inflation grew worse it was common for parcels to be delivered almost entirely covered with a layer of postage stamps. Ziegler carefully saved the great coloured blocks and passed them onto his nephew Gustav, Lotte's brother Albert's teenage son. "The boy will soon be able to paper the walls of his room with those things," Albert had said. "You know, he sometimes just sits there and stares at them, all laid out on the floor or on his bed. Don't know what he sees in them—they're only stamps, after all. Still, I suppose it keeps him out of mischief."

Ziegler started to wonder if giving the stamps away had been a sensible thing to do after all. Perhaps it wasn't only him who could see the patterns, and how they were trying to break out of the coloured blocks of paper. Once he had started to notice them, he saw them all the time, and had thought that not being given the opportunity to see them would solve the problem. Instead, perhaps he was making things worse. But he couldn't suddenly and without explanation stop giving Gustav the stamps. Perhaps he should break the blocks down into smaller ones before he gave them away . . .

He had first become aware of the patterns when he opened a parcel of corrected proofs. Apart from the addresses, there had been almost none of the wrapping paper to be seen. Instead the parcel was covered in pale brown postage stamps which had in turn been overprinted with an even higher value. The ranked rows of solid black overprints—Ziegler noted with astonishment that each was for four hundred thousand marks—danced in front of his eyes before each receded with great speed so that he seemed to be gazing down at a grating or lattice beneath which was a tiny but infinitely deep shaft or pit. The postmarks had slid away from the overprints. He quickly looked under his

85

Ziegler Against the World

desk and to his relief saw only the solid wooden floor. He looked up again, to check if anyone else in the office had noticed what he had done. He had not been observed. He stared at the parcel on his desk. Perhaps the tiny black holes extended all the way down to the centre of the planet, or to hell. He shook his head and the apparition cleared away. All that Ziegler had in front of him was a parcel—no more and no less. The stamps covering them were merely a second paper skin, a patchwork of colours and black overprints.

"Well, open it, man!" Herr Fuchs said irritably, leaning over Gerold's desk. "I've been waiting for him to send those proofs back. Tell me, are you feeling all right, Herr Ziegler?" For a moment Fuchs looked at him with genuine concern. "Come now, unwrap that parcel and give it to me. Then go down into the courtyard for a few minutes and get some air. Perhaps you are working here too late and too often."

Ziegler folded up the wrapping paper. The stamps were just as they should have been. He slipped on his jacket and went downstairs. Perhaps he had been working too hard at the translation. It had so often been a way to avoid dwelling on the dreams, as if the now familiar text were a talisman to be invoked or a spell to be recited. He could escape into Huysmans' words, even as he worked at transmuting them into his own language, even as he laboured to keep the essence of the original. Perhaps the very words themselves, what they were and what they stood for, were changing within his mind, being refined into something else, clear and pure, to show him the way he wanted to travel, if only he could grasp it. If only he could take Lotte with him then he would have no qualms. As it was, maybe he should proceed more slowly with the work. He remembered his dreams and the sense of a resolution to come when he finished his task. That was as frightening as it was alluring. He went back upstairs to his desk.

A Flowering Wound

❦

Lotte briskly picked up the mound of wrapping paper and envelopes, all plastered over with stamps, which Ziegler had accumulated and brought home for Gustav. He had deliberately left them where Lotte could not avoid seeing them. She had ignored them for most of the evening before laughing and dropping them onto Gerold's lap. She was sure he shuddered for the briefest moment before smiling as he stuffed the stamps into an old envelope. For his part Ziegler was glad Lotte showed no indication she had noticed any of the patterns and signs that he now saw all the time.

No-one in the office seemed to have noticed them either, any more than Gustav or his father had said anything when Gerold had taken the last pile of stamps round to their apartment, letting them slide out of the envelope and onto the worn tablecloth in a multi-coloured avalanche. Gustav had whistled in pleasure and started to sort through the stamps. He hadn't seemed to see what Gerold saw. It was the way overprinted stamps had been placed on a parcel, assuming the form of a hieroglyph or a letter from an unknown alphabet, or how blocks of different coloured stamps revealed themselves to be city blocks on a map of a hidden, secret town that he might be able to reach one day, or as the setting for a strange chess-like game for which the pieces, moves, and forfeits—all the rules—were as yet hidden from him and the world. Now Ziegler's eyes could flicker over the values printed on the stamps and instantly add them to produce colossal numbers with even more of a life of their own than they had as money. He was sure each of the great numbers with their comet-tails of zeros must have significances of their own not as yet revealed to him.

He kept his thoughts from his wife, their families and friends. At present they were for him alone. If anyone else

Ziegler Against the World

was to be let into the secret, Ziegler would be informed. There was still only one person with whom he wished to talk about it all, and the only one he was sure was worthy: the dead French soldier he had buried only those few years earlier. By now Ziegler had stopped needing to refer to the copy of the book he'd taken and preserved. He kept it away from Lotte, securely locked in his desk at the office. In any case he had absorbed the text. He knew it intimately and it came to him; he could recall it all whenever he wished.

Meanwhile as he worked or relaxed the words were always there, in French or German—the German words wavering as if seen through running water, varying their meanings slightly while also remaining constant like the bed of the stream beneath. Ziegler continued with his translation, amending and amending again as the words glowed into life, burned bright, and faded away before being replaced. He made very slow progress: he did not hold himself back, but could not go fast ahead either. Something drove him on and something else urged him to caution. In his dreams the postage stamps' rouletted edges were serried lines of bared teeth in jaws clamped together, waiting to spring open and tear him to pieces; yet the zeros whispered that he could be the first prophet of the new order that would burst forth out of the earth when he completed his translation and put it out into the world.

"I'll make a special effort and finish it when the inflation has been brought under control," he told himself and once said out loud to Lotte.

But he was also full of apprehension. If the inflation could be tamed then the signs and patterns that were constantly revealing themselves to him would retreat once more, leaving him to sink back into a grey life in the echoing city where he could never escape from the heavy postage

88

A Flowering Wound

stamp grid of its streets and squares, where he would have to resume his contentment there in the warm and smothering care of those who loved him.

"I sometimes think all these stamps are taking you over, drowning you," Lotte said. "What a waste of paper! I can hardly remember the time when you just needed to stick the one little bit of paper on a letter or parcel, can you? That was all it took, wasn't it, Gerold? And it was delivered exactly to the right place and on time?"

"Yes, Lotte, you are right," Gerold said, smiling as he looked up at her. She was partially silhouetted in front of the one table lamp they were using in the room. He blinked in the light, dim though it was, as she moved out of its way. It was an eclipse coming to an end. "It's hard to remember the normal times any more. But these other times cannot last for ever. They will come to an end, I suppose." He dropped the envelope full of stamps onto the floor by his armchair. "I'll take those round for Gustav tomorrow evening," he said.

❧

In the morning Gerold couldn't remember dreaming. Lotte was pleased that he hadn't awoken from a nightmare. But he was sure he must have dreamed. There was no reason for the dreams to have stopped.

When he noticed his colleagues preparing to go home Ziegler put his papers away and went to get his coat and hat.

"Not staying late tonight?" Herr Fuchs said. "I'm glad you're not overdoing it, but you don't want to fall behind with your translation either, do you? It must be nearly finished by now!"

Ziegler shook his head. "I have to take some things round to my brother-in-law's place," he said.

Ziegler Against the World

It was foggy outside. A pearly halo surrounded each streetlight. On both sides the huge buildings reached up into the fog. The street was a dank grey corridor. For a moment Ziegler stood on the kerb, hesitating. He pictured himself at his desk again, his copy of *Là-Bas* in front of him but unopened. Although he no longer needed it, he still kept it. Its words were the only true ones, visible and genuine, black on white. He imagined starting to rework one of the passages he'd already translated, writing swiftly from memory, the German flowing out of him easily and onto the page as he thought the French must have done years before. Ziegler almost turned and went back inside, but stopped himself.

His colleague Rainer almost bumped into him. "We're going for a beer," he said. "Come for a beer, just the one. It's been a long time." Ziegler shook his head. He could afford to buy a glass of beer, and Lotte wouldn't mind—but he wanted to get away.

"Forgive me. I can't, not this evening. Maybe next time."

Rainer grinned, pulled up the collar of his overcoat, and strolled off into the mist. Ziegler walked on after him, slowly. He decided to walk all the way home instead of waiting for the tram in Friedrichstrasse. He wanted to clear his head. Despite the cold and the fog closing in he felt that being outside in the street would help keep the words at bay for a while, at least. And in the mist there would be no signs, no patterns: nothing to distract or influence him.

Ziegler walked carefully, avoiding the shapes of other pedestrians as they loomed out of the fog. It was now full night. He looked down at the pavement, anxious not to trip over any uneven stones or miss his footing and fall into the road. He made sure there were no cars or bicyclists anywhere near him—that he could see—before venturing to cross the street.

A Flowering Wound

It was when he paused in one of the small curving streets on the other side of the river that he first noticed the smell. He sniffed. A blur hurrying past called out *"Gesundheit!"* Ziegler sniffed again, several times. Now he was sure of it: smoke. In the deserted street there was no sign of anything burning, nor could he hear any shouts or screams. He couldn't hear the fire brigade. He resumed his walking, heading past the cliffs of the Town Hall glowing softly in the gloom, on towards Alexanderplatz. He couldn't shake off the taint of smoke; he also tasted it faintly, as if someone nearby were continually striking matches.

Reaching Alexanderplatz Ziegler navigated around the edge of the bustling and crowded space. He still smelled smoke. A smouldering brazier, surrounded by workmen, was an infernal sign. It seemed inevitable for him to en-counter smoke and flame—on the surface. He went out of his way to avoid the yawning pits and piles of rubble and churned-up soil where the new Underground station was taking shape. Light filtered out from the windows of shops and the great department store, casting edgeless shadows and barely illuminating a path through the fog and smoke. Large brightly-lit squares and rectangles floated in the swirling grey vapours like blocks of garish postage stamps; like entrances to another place.

Ziegler left Alexanderplatz behind and plunged back into the surrounding tangle of narrow streets and courtyards. Soon the street widened in front of him and he began to trudge up the drawn-out and gentle slope leading out of the city's heart towards his home. He could still smell smoke, and the foggy air itself now seemed to pulse with an inner glow that saturated everything around him: apartment blocks, churches, trees, vehicles, the road, and the pavement he walked on. The wall of a block of flats rippled as he walked past; Ziegler touched the damp stucco and it felt slimy. The wall flowed again under his hand before becoming still and rigid once more. He began to sway slightly as the pavement began to undulate, the tiny cubes of stone at the edge by the road moving up and down in their places by two or three millimetres. It was as if he were walking on the back of a gigantic creature that was beginning to wake up. He coughed in the smoke. Flames crackled and roared in the distance. Ziegler stopped walking and looked around him. Passers-by seemed unaware of anything unusual, and the traffic flowed by as it always did.

The last thing he wanted was to draw attention to himself or do anything that could cause a policeman to stop and ask questions. He turned his back on the street and pretended to study the display in the window of a florist's shop. He wished he could afford one of the large bunches of flowers as a surprise for Lotte. There was a movement behind him, caught in the glass. He turned and gasped as the kerbstones broke free from the pavement and reared up, the stone cubes dropping and sliding into place as blunt, worn teeth. The expanding mouth exhaled smoky breath; its fumes mixed with the fog.

Ziegler backed away and felt behind him, touching the window of the flower-shop. It was blessedly cold and solid. He moved sideways until he felt the wooden frame beneath his fingers, while all the time his gaze was held by the kerb opening itself up as if in a yawn. The mouth didn't move any closer. He thought about the sharp teeth of the postage stamps and zeros in his dreams, and for an instant wondered if he could wake himself up to find that he was sitting at his desk, or even still lying in bed. He could hit his head against the building, but that would mean he had to turn away from the mouth and let it out of his sight.

The pavement swelled further. The mouth grew wider and its square teeth began to form into sharply-pointed

A Flowering Wound

ones. A gap appeared in the fog and smoke, and for a moment Ziegler saw across to the other side of the wide street where a stout man waited to cross. His hands were thrust deep into his pockets, his dark coat and jacket were wide open; he stood like a statue. Light glinted off the watch-chain stretching across the expanse of the man's waistcoat. Ziegler thought about the fine watch and chain he had, all gold and silver; he rarely wore it because he couldn't bear to think of losing it or having it stolen from him. Then he remembered something that he did have with him.

On his wedding day Lotte's father had given him a half mark piece: a gleaming silver coin that had never seen use. It could have been fresh from the mint. "You won't get these again in a hurry," his new father-in-law had said. "They're already vanishing. Look at that. Our country's name is the same but everything else has changed. Keep it for luck. Maybe things will go back to the way they used to be, when we all knew where we were." Gerold had known what Herr Thalberg meant. Lotte's father supported the restoration of the Monarchy, and only tolerated the Republic while wishing it would be swept away. He blamed it for the inflation and the loss of his savings. Over beer in his local bar he would sometimes tell Gerold and Albert that Germany was a body stretched out on a rack, with foreigners and outsiders extorting every last real mark and pfennig, every last drop of blood from the battered corpse. "But corpses can be made to come to life again," he would mutter. Albert would roll his eyes while Gerold wandered what he really wanted to happen.

Ziegler always kept the coin in the watch pocket of his waistcoat. Now he carefully reached in and plucked it out. It was a small, light coin, but it now had more sway and greater power than a pile of banknotes. The coin glinted in his hand. Regretfully he knew what to do. He threw the

Ziegler Against the World

coin into the gaping mouth. It hit one of the razor teeth with a sound that he heard as a striking bell. The coin didn't fly back out onto the pavement, but slipped down between the smoking jaws and into the flickering darkness. Suddenly the mouth sucked itself in and disappeared; the mist lay undisturbed on the damp pavement and kerb as if nothing had happened. The man opposite had reached Ziegler's side of the street and was lighting a cigar. A woman came out of the florist's. Ziegler knelt down and pretended to check his shoelaces before resuming his walk home.

Later that evening Lotte found her husband had opened the envelope of stamps and spread them out over the floor, where they formed a shape that seemed strangely familiar. Then she realised why that was: in front of her lay Germany. Gerold seemed dazed and shook his head. "Yes, you're right, Lotte, so it is," he said. "Strange. I wonder how that happened." He began to gather the stamps up again. "It's too late to go out now, and I'm rather tired after my walk home. I'll have to give them to Gustav another day."

❧

Rumours began to spread that the Government and the Reichsbank had finally come up with a plan to end the hyperinflation once and for all. There was something about a new but temporary currency with its own bank to administer it. When Ziegler heard the reports the words inside him sang in a jumble of French and German that the time was drawing near. They urged him to bring his translation to an end. His dreams stopped waking him up in terror. The words held out a freedom to him: his life would become fully his own again, and the new *Là-Bas* would make Gerold Ziegler a man to be reckoned with. He would be on the way to becoming a rich man. All Germans

A Flowering Wound

had got used to dealing with amounts of money where the zeros had multiplied beyond control and meaning; he could continue to enjoy a good few zeros for real, where they counted.

The zeros still haunted him. Ziegler couldn't get them out of his mind. The yawning mouths, the teeth—their enormous numbers which for him could only be paralleled by the number of the war dead, the quantity of bullets and shells manufactured and fired, and the very money spent on conducting the war. All still infected and controlled the aftermath. To him the zeros and the words were part of a world that he now knew beyond doubt to have been thrown out of balance since he had picked up and taken on the copy of *Là-Bas*. The dreams, the patterns and signs, the zeros, the crunching teeth: there was only one way to banish them—if they would be banished.

Ziegler had not taken any holiday leave during the summer just past, so he asked for a week's leave of absence. His request was granted. He made sure he had plenty of paper, pens, and ink. He told Lotte that he was going to complete the translation and that would be an end to it. He brought the French copy of *Là-Bas* home and put it on the table in front of him, next to the pile of scribbled sheets and fair copies that formed his unfinished translation.

"Write neater if you want me to copy it without making any mistakes," Lotte said.

"We can worry about that afterwards," he replied.

Lotte went out to do some shopping while Gerold arranged and rearranged everything on the table. Then the words told him to stop and listen to them. That Monday was spent in going through the part of his translation that he had already committed to paper. The words approved and congratulated; they criticised and prompted final changes. When he finally went to bed he slept soundly.

95

Ziegler Against the World

On the second day the words again told him to listen carefully and write. He recognised phrases and fragments in the clamour of French and German as the words talked to each other and edited themselves, agreeing and arguing, before making themselves available to Ziegler's pen. By the time it grew dark outside the windows his arms and eyes ached; his back was painful and his legs numb. But the pile of fair copy stacked on the table was higher than it had been before.

On the third day the words chattered about the zeros. The Government had announced that the new temporary currency would be introduced the next day, coming into effect at the rate of one to a trillion. Ziegler got very little written; the words told him they would make it up and finish the following day. Ziegler had his first nightmare of the week: screaming zeros consuming each other before pursuing him through the streets to his flat.

Lotte had no idea what was happening in her husband's mind while he slept. His body remained almost completely motionless. As the battle erupted Ziegler sat at his desk in the office listening to his colleagues discussing the increasing bizarre events being reported from across the country.

Men and women wept as the handfuls of banknotes they were clutching faded into thin air. The secret patterns of postage stamps and overprints rearranged themselves as people stared at them; the new symbols brought out hidden meanings in the letters and newspapers that the stamps had been wrapped around. Zeros hovered in the air and lay on the pavements, swallowing up pedestrians and sometimes whole vehicles. From the Oberbaumbrücke the Spree ran dry as the river was gulped down by a cloud of zeros that had floated on the current before stopping at the bridge and opening themselves.

A Flowering Wound

The rite whispered itself in the brown and brittle leaves in parks and on pavements as a single tremendous ceremony rolled out over the Reich. In Köln multiplications of zeros as fat as bagels were flinging themselves over the great spires and innumerable pinnacles of the Cathedral, sliding down onto them in a gigantic game of Ringwerfen. In Weimar copies of the Constitution appeared out of the sky and fluttered around aimlessly before splitting into their separate pages, growing pointed beaks and flying off to Leipzig to hurl themselves at the windows of the Supreme Court building. Clouds of billion mark banknotes were reported drifting over Stuttgart, Hannover, and Königsberg; they swirled down and settled—paper snow that caused chaos in the streets.

A row of glistening white teeth a metre high thrust up out of the soil along the new frontier with Poland near Schneidemühl. Along parts of the Czechoslovak and Austrian borders teeth broke through and cracked open roads and lifted sections of railway track; the documents of people waiting to cross became slices of salami which turned slimy and disintegrated within seconds. A drift of banknotes dammed the Kiel Canal, while zeros a metre in diameter rolled through the streets of Potsdam and Regensburg, swerving from side to side and crushing anybody and anything in their paths. Sheets of fifty milliard mark postage stamps glued themselves to the windows of the cavernous reading room of the Prussian State Library in Unter den Linden and draped themselves over the dome and walls of St. Hedwig's Cathedral. The interiors of both buildings quickly descended into deep twilight. Zeros hung on the statue of the angel on top of the Victory Column outside the Reichstag building like pretzels on a stick; an office boy ran in and shouted that the golden statue had toppled from its place and crashed into the square below.

Ziegler Against the World

Sitting at his desk Ziegler saw the readers in the State Library blundering into shelves and desks and each other in the inky darkness after the electric light failed. All over the vast building matches and cigarette lighters were produced. In the flickering dimness Professor Tiedemann twisted together a handful of ten million mark notes to make a torch. The paper screamed, its zeros yawning wide as they charred and crumbled away. The professor swore and dropped the flaming banknotes onto the manuscript he had been consulting. The fire caught even as the old man ponderously tried to separate the pages and extinguish the burning ones. He swore again and flung the manuscript away from him as he burnt his fingers. Smouldering pages drifted like scintillating galaxies in the high black space under the dome and ignited everything they touched. The reading room rapidly became a vortex of flame, the smoke rising up and joining with other columns of smoke to hide the sky over the entire city behind a choking blanket. The sun faded out as ash and fragments of charred paper began to fall, silently and softly, out of the sky.

In the office dusk had fallen. Outside the window the air was becoming thick with smoke and ash. The sky was a solid charcoal grey, stretched taut like a drum. Close to the horizon the sky flickered from time to time. They reminded Ziegler of the sparks discharging from electrical apparatus, except they must have been kilometres long. People lay in the street where they had fallen after breathing in the congested air. The telephones stopped ringing, and when Dr. Ritter tried to get a connection to one of their suppliers in Breslau there were no voices to be heard. All he could pick up was what sounded like the faint whistling of a distorted version of the national anthem.

Ziegler tried to wake up but couldn't move. Although he could pace from his desk to the office window and back

A Flowering Wound

again, his sleeping body remained entirely motionless. Lotte slept on next to him, undisturbed. The words spoke to him within his dream. The French words and phrases rumbled beneath the German ones. Soon Ziegler realised that the French *Là-Bas* was very slowly drowning out its German version—his own sentences that he had been releasing onto paper during the majority of his waking hours.

He went to his desk and unlocked the drawer where he kept his copy of the novel. Its silk binding was just as he remembered it, down to the tiny stain where the book had got wet when he'd picked it up from the grass. He flicked through the pages, running his fingers over the thin crisp paper and gazing at the clear sharp font and decorations. Letters, words, and sentences blurred and stained his hands. He forced the book wide open, pushing its covers back towards each other so they were moved to an embrace over the cracking spine. He dropped the limp book into his waste paper basket.

"Please would you lend me your cigarette lighter, Herr Fuchs?" he said.

Black smoke boiled outside the window, leavened by flashes of orange fire. Everyone in the office gathered around Gerold's desk. He took a ten million mark note from his wallet, lit it, and dropped it into the basket. The book caught fire, releasing clouds of black smoke which filled the office. They started to cough. Ziegler dropped the rest of his money into the waste paper basket so that flames shot out over its rim.

Ziegler walked to the window, and pushed it open, letting the smoky air inside mix with the smoke billowing outside. The French words died away and the German ones diminished to a whisper before fading away altogether. Ziegler and everyone in the office coughed and spluttered uncontrollably, throwing themselves around and hitting themselves against the walls and furniture. An arm flailed and struck him in the face, knocking him over. His nose started to bleed. Blood spurted out over his shirt. He wiped his hands on it. Crawling back to his waste paper basket he leaned over it, breathing in more smoke and feeling heat of the dying fire on his face. A single flame leapt up and singed his eyebrows, but his blood flowed and doused the fire. He breathed in smoke and embers; blood clotted in his nose and trickled into his throat, and he began to choke. He closed his eyes and waited, convulsed.

Ziegler woke up with a start. He thought a scream or whisper must have woken him. He strained to hear the sounds he was expecting to hear, but there was nothing. His throat was dry and he couldn't taste or smell anything. Eyes still shut he took a careful breath and cautiously touched his nose. There was no pain or sign of blood. Lotte stirred and touched his arm. "I'm all here," he said.

The apartment was silent except for the morning noises filtering in through the walls. Ziegler opened his eyes and padded over to the window. Outside the sky was clear and the city exhaled no more smoke and fumes than usual. Today the zeros were to be cut down to size and numbers would become sensible and manageable once more. He looked forward to returning to work. He wanted to examine everything on the way. And there was one thing still to do, something he hadn't quite finished: he couldn't be certain as to what it was, but he would surely remember soon.

The blocks of postage stamps piled on the carpet by his armchair caught his attention, but something split apart in his mind and dropped away like threads fraying and separating in a tapestry. The design or pattern dwindled

A Flowering Wound

down into the meaningless. Lotte's mouth formed an "O" of surprise as Gerold sat down for breakfast wearing his suit, dressed for work. As she smiled at him he noticed that her teeth looked rather sharp.

A Flowering Wound

I open to you like a flowering wound,
or a trough in the sea filled with dreaming fish,
or a steaming chasm of earth
split by a major quake.

You changed the topography.
Where valleys were,
there are now mountains.
Where deserts were,
there now are seas.

– Erica Jong, "After the Earthquake"

I t's when I uncover his head. The man must have almost made it out as the building collapsed: there is hardly any rubble on top of him, but his legs are pinned under a concrete lintel and his head is covered by part of a shattered door. That is how I find the man, clawing away at bricks and concrete with my bare hands as the others all around are doing. Then I recognise his hand from the wristwatch. I pull the wood away from his head. I am surrounded by sobs and cries, the shouts of commands and curses. Floodlights and torches shine over the debris: searching eyes hovering over it. The man's eyes are closed, his face and hair covered in dust. There is a trickle of blood, already dried. But his head moves slightly and he is breathing. I resist the impulse

102

A Flowering Wound

to try to brush flakes of concrete and brick dust off his face and cradle the man in my arms. In any case his feet are still buried by concrete blocks and chunks of wood. I turn away, shout for help.

For a moment I'm dazzled by a torch. It flickers into my eyes and then plays on his face.

"You've found someone?" Radu says. He points the torch again and kneels down beside me, bending in close.

"He's still alive," I manage to say.

"He's a fucking Yid," Radu says. "Can't you tell? Half the apartments in this place were Yid apartments. We hadn't got them all out yet. Now it's too late anyway, eh?"

I lean in, trying to put myself between the man and Radu. In case he speaks; his mouth is trying to move, to open and form words.

"It'll be all right," I whisper.

"Leave that," Radu shouts. "No, wait."

Radu pushes me out of the way and smashes the torch against the man's forehead. The light goes out, but not before I see that his mouth stops trying to open.

"Sorted," Radu says. "The carcass can be dealt with later. There's still plenty of Romanians to save yet."

The man—the man's name is (was; no, it must be is) Sebastian. His apartment high in the Charlton Building is white and clean; the Boulevard seems so far below that a different air and sunlight applies. He puts a book back on the white shelves.

"So is it because I am Sebastian Vidranu, that Yid who has a flat in the exclusive Charlton Building in Brătianu Boulevard, and I'm sleeping with you, and we both enjoy it? So that means I'm assimilated, I'm really as Romanian as you and your friends are, after all? Please, Mihai!" He sits down opposite me. "You're better than that! Aren't you? Do you think that you make up for some sort of defect I have,

A Flowering Wound

fill in a cavity, make me one hundred per cent human? Is that it? Yes, Mihai, you've rubbed off on me all right, you know that, don't you? You have. Is that what this is about? Have you decided you're sorry?"

I stand up and make as if I'm leaving. The man turns his head to look at the wall of books ranked row upon row.

"Yes!" I shout. "To all of that. But I don't mind. I know I'm a Romanian. The Legion is right. We need a national cleansing and renewal. Anyone, anything, who is not one of us, who is against the nation—"

"So what am I then, Mihai?" he shouts back. "Can you answer that? You're here, aren't you? What am I then? Is something wrong or am I ill? Or is it maybe you needing to be cured of what you are?"

The earthquake strikes in the early hours of a November morning. It lasts nearly five minutes. Houses, offices, shops, churches cave in and fold up all over Bucharest. When the earth is quiet again the most prominent casualty is the Charlton Building, the tallest apartment block in the city and a stunning example of the modernist style in architecture. Dominating the Boulevard, the complex includes offices and a cinema. The brightly-lit future is brought to us in a ruled majestic line of sleek white structures cutting sharply through the irregular streets and gardens of the old city.

The rescue attempt is a dismal failure. Immediately the tremors finish fading away, German military engineers stationed in the city offer to help. But with pockets of air becoming exhausted and water mains flooding the basement under the enormous pile of wreckage that is all that is left of the tower block, our Legionary leaders insist on us doing the work ourselves, and mainly with our bare hands. Some have shovels to begin with if they're lucky. We waste our time.

A Flowering Wound

The gendarme doesn't even bother to try and shoot at me as we run. He eventually gives up the chase and falls behind. Winded, panting for breath and covered in sweat, I find myself on the Boulevard, sprinting along it and keeping close to the buildings lining its clean empty length. It seems safer than any of the streets leading into it. Then I hear shouts and more firing and I dodge into a deeply recessed doorway. The man is standing on the other side of the thick engraved glass doors, solidly set into their ornate brass and bronze frame. We make eye contact for a moment: that is all. The door is as unmoving as a wall, as the pillars supporting the concrete tower soaring above. I almost bounce out onto the pavement again, but I look back over my shoulder and see the door opening slowly. He beckons me inside.

Later Sebastian says that he has not left his apartment for several days. He is prepared: the place is well-stocked with food and drink. His servant is back in Cluj until things calm down again. He offers to sew up the tears in my jacket himself; he says his father once taught him the basics of the trade. I empty the pockets and a Legionary medallion falls out and clatters across the polished inlaid table.

"I wonder why that didn't fall out earlier," Sebastian says. I pick it up and look again at the profile of the Captain on the face and the outline of the country shaped on the reverse. The light glances off its bright clean surface.

"He is a great man," I say reverently. "I met him once. His time will come."

Sebastian starts to work. Then he says, "I think there's something I need to make clear to you." He bites off a length of thread and puts the needle away.

Radu knocks back another plum brandy and says, "What happened to you?"

I start to explain, but he grins and hands me a full glass. "Drink that," he laughs. "Maybe you haven't heard, then.

A Flowering Wound

We've got Carol scared. He's holed up in the palace. He might think he doesn't need us, but we certainly don't need him. We'll soon sweep him away, with his Jewish clique and the rest of them."

Someone makes a joke about Magda Lupescu, King Carol's mistress. Loud laughter echoes around the tiny overheated room, and I join in. But some of us are missing. Soon we will hold the roll-call, when we will hail the martyrs' names, crying out the responses, making them proudly.

I drink, fingering the medallion in my pocket. I can't tell which of the raised textured surfaces I feel between my finger and thumb are which: the Captain or the country. It doesn't matter. They are one, the dead and the living, and I am with them and them in me.

When King Carol abdicates in September and the National Legionary State is declared, Legionaries are taken into the Government and we go on to the streets in celebration. We have endured months of national humiliation, losing territory to the Bolsheviks, to Hungary, to Bulgaria. Carol and his camarilla escape from the nation they leave betrayed and mutilated. But we perform our own recompenses.

Sebastian says he has to find 75,000 lei or leave his apartment. I turn away from the balcony. "I'm afraid I can't—"

He jumps up from the Bauhaus sofa, comes over to where I'm standing. Behind me he rests his hands on my shoulders. "I know. I'm not asking you," he says. I can feel the man's warm breath on the back of my neck; I smell his cologne and stray traces of the expensive imported bourbon we are both drinking. "The money is no problem. I can raise it. You know why it's getting more and more difficult to remain here. István isn't ever coming back from Cluj—I told him it's too dangerous for him here. You know why that is." Sebastian kisses the back of my neck. "But I don't

A Flowering Wound

want to leave, do I? There's someone who makes me want to stay. Anyway, I was born in Bucharest. I have a lovely home here. I have a right—"

"You have no rights," I say to myself, moving my lips but not making a sound. "No, I don't want you to leave here," I say. "But that's when I'm here, up in the air." Sebastian begins to laugh gently. Then his broad shoulders start heaving as he laughs harder and louder. The man says he doesn't want to tell me why he's laughing so much; why he finds it so funny.

I start to say that it's not only when I'm with him in the apartment, but all I do is to stop his laughter with my mouth.

I ask Radu what happened to the bodies found in the rubble after the earthquake.

"They were disposed of correctly," he says. "You've seen we know how to look after our own, and to do it well. Other Romanians were buried with only the rites of Holy Orthodox Church. Other Christians by their rites, I suppose. And as for anyone else—" Radu stops suddenly and puts his glass down, still half full of spirit. He looks me straight in the eye; through me, I feel. "You're thinking about the Charlton Building, aren't you? About when you were doing your bit with the rescue work."

Radu still stares at me. For a moment his face assumes a distracted, almost vacant gaze, as if the mind behind it, looking out of the eyes, is turning its attention away; then it comes back almost at once. "Mihai, I know what this is about. It's that Yid you found, isn't it? Was that the first corpse you'd ever seen? I think I envy you!" He calls for more brandy, and slops some into my glass. "Do you really want to know what happened to those corpses? I don't think it was nice. I could ask around. But why are you so

A Flowering Wound

interested, Mihai? Anyone would think that you knew the man or something. Hey, you didn't, did you?" Radu bellows with laughter at the absurdity of it.

I forget how many times I deny it.

I stand on the pavement, staring at the ruins of the Charlton Building. The mountain of rubble has been cleared away; only the walls of the cinema and a few shattered concrete pillars are still standing. Scavengers pick through the scoured earth and surround a bonfire. The Boulevard is busy with people and traffic. Workmen scurry around; the exposed wall of the apartment block next to the site is being propped up with massive wooden supports, and cracks are being examined minutely. Furniture and suitcases are piled up on the pavement: the tenants are being moved out as a precaution.

I continue walking north along the Boulevard, towards Piaţa Romană. The white canyon of modern buildings is becoming grey and dusty; smooth white walls are cracked and pitted, exposing concrete frames and brick fillings. I wander the streets around the Boulevard and Calea Victoriei, and all the way back down to the river. I try to lose myself in the city, but it isn't possible. I know the bars and cafés, parks and street corners all too well. At ground level the future is stalled, mired in mud and cobbles. It is as much my city as Sebastian's; I tell myself I am part of building it up, making it worthy of the renewed society we strive for. I cross the Boulevard again and again, backwards and forwards, ignoring the traffic and the way people look at me. A tram narrowly misses me; I step back on the rail but the tram is gone, leaving behind gasps, and cries of derision and fright. For hours I wear tracks into the pavements, slowly and deliberately rubbing the tangled printed plan off the map. I am hiding Bucharest as I penetrate it further. I

A Flowering Wound

rub it out, I dream of pulling it down as the hours slide into twilight. I can no longer bear to go home or to the Legion House. I am back at the ruins of the Charlton Building again when a voice makes me stand still.

"Mihai."

I stare at the man.

"Mihai, are you all right?" he says. "What's wrong? Don't you know who I am? It's me." He takes hold of my arm and starts to pull me slowly along the pavement. "Come on, let's go home to the House and have a drink," he says. "You'll be among your friends again."

I say the man's name, and immediately don't remember which one comes out. My legs blossom with pain, cracking as they give way under crushing weight. I cough and choke. The skin and bone of my left temple splits in an agonising budding of blood. As the darkness sweeps in, my mouth opens and I bloom in a flower of concrete fragments and brick dust, voicelessly spreading, spreading.

We, the Rescued

We, the rescued,
We press your hand
We look into your eye—
But all that binds us together is leave-taking

– Nelly Sachs

"I dream of heat," Sean said. "I long for it." Light and warmth were always in short supply during the depths of a north European winter. He had thought he would be used to it. But not this time: everything was different.

Sean had moved to Berlin the previous summer. He had told himself it was now or never. Whether or not it was because of what he only half-jokingly referred to as his mid-life crisis, a feeling of restlessness and an ache for change had overwhelmed him. He had felt there was no longer anything—or anyone—to keep him in England. His German friends had encouraged him to take the leap. According to them the employment opportunities for native English speakers with excellent German language skills and cultural knowledge had never been better.

And he loved Berlin. Over the years he had paid many visits, both for work and pleasure—and frequently having the chance to mix the two. The great, brash city, sprawling over the wide face of the land, had never palled on him. He relished the broad avenues, channels through the massed buildings, their vanishing-points shimmering in the heat-haze. He wandered the city's intricate net of alleyways and footpaths, savoured the innumerable little cafés and bars nestling in the ground floors of apartment buildings, and made notes on the unexpected statues and memorials in its squares and parks. He had gradually woven them all, his Berlin, into a fabric that he could roll out across the empty spaces that more and more often seemed to be in wait for him when he let down his guard. Every time he was alone again the spaces seemed to have swallowed a larger part of him, spreading out in an endless dull stain and wiping out what he knew he should still remember and cherish. As he passed forty, Sean became convinced that only in Berlin, that city of ghosts and the ruins of so many aborted and abandoned futures, could he pick up, fresh and wiped clean, a new future.

When he received an email from his friend Peter telling him that a publishing company specialising in large and glossy art books was recruiting for its Berlin head office, he jumped at the opportunity. Successful, he gave notice on his rented flat in London, and packed away the few possessions he had accumulated over the years. As the plane banked low over the grid of red roofs and trees, all glowing in the afternoon sunshine, he knew that he had done the right thing. The future reared up in front of him, as solid as the approaching airport runway and as open-ended as the wake of a pleasure boat working the River Spree.

Grinning and laughing, Peter and his partner Matthias shook Sean's hand, before driving to a bar in Prenzlauer Berg that he already knew. They sat outside, watching the cars and trams glide past as the buttery yellow light began to fade from the walls of the apartment blocks. Light spilled across pavements, and shadows deepened under the trees. Somewhere

We, the Rescued

above a band started to practice, the drums' beat drizzling down through the warm smoky air like drops of sound rain.

A slim, fair-haired man in a worn and faded denim jacket walked past. Matthias nudged Sean, grinning. "Too young for you!"

Sean smiled and nodded. He sat back in his chair. The remainder of the past slid away. This new future had better be good: it would have to last him for the rest of his life.

Sean had a week of grace before his new job began. Matthias and Peter had agreed to let him stay in their spare room until he could find a place of his own. The next morning he set up his laptop on their kitchen table and started to search for rooms or apartments for rent. The kitchen window was open to the hot morning air; empty blue sky burned overhead. Sunlight glanced off the white walls and reflected in the glossy kitchen units. Below, the heavy door from the entrance hall into the courtyard slammed; there was a burst of laughter.

"As it's your first day I will grind the coffee," Peter had said. The aroma filled the room. Sean sipped the dark and scalding liquid. He registered his interest on several websites, thinking as he did so about the parts of Berlin where he would like to live—and where he could afford to live. Not too far out: certainly not one of the massive housing estates on the edge. Not somewhere that needed renovation. Not somewhere overlooking a motorway . . . His phone sang. It was Matthias.

"We see you for lunch, Sean. There is a friend, a good guy, we want you to meet him."

They arranged to meet in a café close to Arnimplatz, on the other side of Schönhauser Allee. It was a short walk from his friends' apartment. Even as he ended the call Sean's stomach churned in anticipation. He got up and rinsed out his coffee mug and cleaned the breakfast things.

112

A Flowering Wound

The three men were sitting around a small round table. A fourth chair had been pulled out slightly, and left waiting. Matthias caught sight of Sean and waved at him. He navigated his way through the tables. The room was a narrow box of light and talk; the pale wood of the floor seemed to be warm, buoyant. It was hot, even though the street and courtyard doors were open.

Matthias rose to his feet and pointed at the empty chair. He and Peter shook Sean's hand. "Sean, this is our friend Kai," Peter said. Then the third man also got up and held out his hand.

Sean wasn't very hungry, but ate some salad. They drank icy pale beer. Sean glanced at his friends, and his new acquaintance. He smiled, as he thought how someone looking at all four of them would think them so similar. Sean knew that he, Matthias, and Peter were all within two years of each other in age, and he guessed Kai was in his early forties as well. They were all in good shape—they took care to look after themselves. "Everything curves, goes in or sticks out as it should!" Peter had once said. Peter's hair had recently turned a consistent and distinguished silver, and Matthias now had to wear glasses for reading, as Sean had done for the past five years. Otherwise their slow move into middle age had been resoundingly tranquil—as far as image was concerned. Carved in silhouette against the glare of the street Kai's profile was sharp, his hair crisp and thick.

"So, Sean," Peter said. "Kai has just come out. He has left it a bit late, but that could not be helped. We two have known the truth since a long time ago!"

Kai nodded, smiling and blushing. He turned to Sean. "It is the best thing."

"Kai is new to Berlin too," Matthias said. "He has just found a nice place to live, but it costs more than he can afford. His money is not, oh, secured just yet. We had an

We, the Rescued

idea. We thought if you liked the apartment as well, you could rent it and Kai could live there as well. He would pay his share."

There were tiny beads of sweat along Kai's hairline, where his scalp was still almost white, even as his face had become tanned. The skin around his brown eyes crinkled as he looked past Sean towards the sunlit street. Sean wanted to take a napkin and gently wipe the moisture away, and touch the delicate skin. It would be warm and silky, he was sure of that. He recalled another of Peter's sayings: "For men like us it is always a market out there." He had agreed. Now he longed to retire from it.

"What do you say, Sean?" Kai asked. "We can go see the apartment? I must give an answer by tonight."

Sean tried to close down his memories of how he'd first met Kai Schierling. He wished he could put them to one side, shove them away—everything except the exhilarating heat and light of the summer, just five months ago. He wanted to recall, to feel, nothing but the warmth.

Sean and Kai had gone to look at the apartment. It was on the second floor of one of the huge and elaborate post-war blocks built as showcase housing along the new Stalinallee—the broad boulevard had long since been re-named Karl-Marx-Allee—and close to the U-Bahn station in Strausberger Platz. The two men wandered through the bare, cool rooms. The apartment had been skilfully refurbished, with the original glass-panelled interior doors and chocolate-brown parquet flooring restored. From the bedroom at the back of the flat Sean saw a panorama of swaying treetops, impaled on church towers like toothpicks. The rooms at the front overlooked the yawning space of the street. From the balcony they could see the fountain in Strausberger Platz. Water glinted, flowing rainbows in the sun.

A Flowering Wound

"Do you like this apartment?" Kai asked anxiously.

"I like it very much. It's just the sort of place I imagined living in when I thought of moving to Berlin." He hesitated. "Shall we rent it?"

When the arrangements had been completed they wandered along the street looking at the shop windows until they found a bar with air conditioning. "I can't imagine ever being cold again," Sean said. "Except in somewhere like this."

"I love the hot weather, don't you?" Kai said.

"Oh yes."

After several cocktails Kai began to talk about himself. He was an interpreter, married, with his wife and teenage daughter still living in the family house in Stuttgart. "I hid my true self for so long," he said. "I did not know. But when I did, I had to leave. Find a new place, get away. But I love my family too—do you understand?"

Sean nodded, but he was not sure that he did—not really.

"I can never break contact with them," Kai continued. "That would be terrible. As long as they want to know me, I must keep a part of myself for them." He swirled the rapidly melting ice in his drink with his straw. "But I won't change again, I won't go back to that way."

Sean looked at his watch. Outside, it was twilight. The bar was filling fast.

Kai leaned over and lightly tapped Sean's wrist. "We are naughty! We have time for another drink. Sex on the Beaches? Two more? Yes, Sean?"

Now Sean couldn't bear the idea of going out to drink cocktails—not by himself, anyway. And the bar still held too many good memories. Although he didn't want to invoke them, he also didn't want to risk wearing them out by rubbing up against them. The heat of the summer months

We, the Rescued

had lasted until almost the end of September, blanketing the city and painting it in brilliant crystal light. He couldn't believe that he had grown used to it, as if there had never been any other Berlin than the city he remembered—living, breathing, and slumbering under a clear Mediterranean sky. Sean wondered if he'd also come to take Kai for granted during that time. He was sure he hadn't, but perhaps there had been *something* he had done or said that had made Kai think differently.

The large bare rooms of the apartment were still sparsely furnished—Sean and Kai had been careful about what they had bought. There had been no hurry. As Sean huddled on their sofa he was no longer sure that the memories he invoked—held out like a shield—of those days of heat and light could prevail against the darkness and cold of December. It was less than a week to Christmas Eve, and Kai had nothing to say about when he would be coming back—or even if he would be returning at all.

Sean felt betrayed in his new and sudden loneliness. Kai had announced that he needed to return to Stuttgart to see his wife and daughter, and clear up some outstanding issues. Sean had started to ask whether it could wait until after Christmas, but stopped himself as he realised that Kai hadn't said that he'd still be away by then.

"It's just temporary, just a few days, Sean," Kai had said. "You know I want to be here with you. But I must go to see Daniela and Ida. Sort things out."

The day Kai had left, Matthias and Peter had flown out to Gran Canaria. They would not be back in Berlin again until the New Year. Then Kai had texted to say he would be away until after Christmas—he was sorry, but it could not be helped. Sean called and called, but Kai's phone remained unanswered.

Alone in the freezing city, Sean tried to act normally, as though nothing had happened. He put in his hours

A Flowering Wound

at work. He tried to ignore the Christmas markets. He brooded on his situation, running through scenario after scenario. Sometimes he believed what Kai had said, and was certain he would return after Christmas, and they could be together again. At other times Sean felt that he couldn't trust Kai, and he wouldn't want him to stay even if he were to return. Then he caught himself, feeling mean and guilty for thinking as he had. He had never been married. He had never had dependents, let alone a child's welfare and future to think about. His own life had been uncomplicated by comparison—he could easily have been accused of selfishness. Then he would feel calm and warm towards Kai . . . but he still did not call or answer his phone. His texts were brief and could have been sent to an acquaintance rather than his lover. Sean resolved that he would wait and see what happened—in any case, he really had no other choice.

The dull, grey chill of the lightless days penetrated him. He found himself shivering at odd moments, even when in warm surroundings and feeling warm. He remembered the apparently endless summer—how he and Kai had taken it for granted as they wrapped themselves in each other, as they touched, coaxed, and scrutinised their bodies into new recognition.

When Sean remembered it was the day of the winter solstice, he cried for a few minutes, embarrassed and guilty, even though there was no-one to see or hear him. Then that realisation made him feel worse, and he sobbed, the hot tears warming his face as he remembered, dream-like, how Kai's also used to, when he had been happy. He looked around their sitting room, its drawn blinds keeping out the night and the lights of the boulevard. He blinked until his tears had cleared from his eyes. The room now had a stark, sharp clarity. Its angles and corners were defined enough to cut at him.

We, the Rescued

Sean was aware of the particular loneliness of a man entering middle age. He had seen it in others, and turned away, afraid. Now he was the man: someone who thought he had finally sorted his life and his relationship, but suddenly could no longer be so sure. There was no longer anywhere safe to walk, nowhere secure to hold on to. And no-one. He did not regret what he had done: the move to Berlin and all the changes that had gone with it. But now, just as he should have been settled, the isolation and gnawing chill had returned.

There had been no new texts from Kai. Sean checked his face in the bathroom mirror, found his coat and scarf, and went down to the icy street. The U-Bahn was noisy and warm, crowded with people returning from work and going to Christmas markets. He got out at Alexanderplatz, and wandered towards the river. The slim shaft of the Television Tower soared from its folded concrete flower, as if frozen and caught in the moment of its creation. The narrow Marien-kirche, standing alone, was brightly lit from within. He saw a poster advertising an organ recital: music for Advent. He remembered that he had wanted to introduce Kai to the Ser-vice of Nine Lessons and Carols broadcast from Cambridge, and explain to him how the ritual of listening to it had come to form the beginning of his Christmas. It was part of the England he had gladly surrendered, but hadn't wanted to lose entirely. Now he decided that it would be appropriate to inaugurate a new ritual and add it to his Christmas habits. As he walked around to the west end of the church, he wondered if he would indeed be here at this time one year hence.

The recital had already begun. Sean slipped into a seat at the back of the church. The audience seemed immersed in the music: tranquillity slowly enveloped him. The organ music filled the space, flowing through it and swallowing up all competing sound. Sean gradually relaxed. Fluttering

A Flowering Wound

applause broke in on his thoughts, and the organist started on the next item. It was an elaborately structured piece that included fragments of a tune that he was sure he had heard before. He looked around for a programme, but decided to stay where he was rather than get up and return to the entrance to look for one. And he didn't want to disturb anyone else by asking about the music. He assumed the strangely familiar tune hidden in the depths of the music was that of one of the traditional German hymns, as leisurely paced and inscrutable as a remote lake in a forest.

Sean tried to appreciate the Advent music, although its melancholy beauty turned him in on himself again, making him gaze at his own longing and expectation. The music was about the light and warmth to come, a celebration—but he had been excluded. He remembered the first Christmas after he had left home, and how he had walked the streets of a different town, looking at the brightly-lit windows of houses, looking in at the warm and decorated rooms as he strode past, and wishing he were in one of those rooms with someone who wanted him there. He wiped his eyes, hoping that he hadn't made any sound during his reverie.

A man sat down next to him, nodding and smiling as if to apologise for any disturbance. Sean smiled back, but found himself glancing at the man over and over again. He knew what he was doing—and in a church, too . . . His new neighbour was ruddy, with high cheekbones and blue eyes. His pale yellow hair, cut short at the sides, was swept back from a wide and clear forehead. He wore a black overcoat and red scarf; although it wasn't cold, he made no attempt to unbutton his coat or remove his scarf. He clutched a charcoal-grey hat and black leather gloves. When he moved his hands Sean noticed several heavy silver rings. There were also flashes of white shirt cuff and a glint of a silver wristwatch or bracelet.

We, the Rescued

Sean tried to keep his mind on the music. He pushed his hands into his coat pockets. For once, he'd forgotten about his phone. He took it out and thumbed the screen, hunching over and trying to make sure no-one could see him. There were no missed calls or text messages. He set the phone to silent and slid it back in his pocket. Every few minutes he pulled it out and checked it, but there were no new notifications. It remained painfully inert.

When the recital ended Sean remained seated. His neighbour stood up. Sean saw that he wore dark blue jeans and highly polished black shoes. Sean felt the man's gaze and looked up at him.

"It is over," he said, smiling. His teeth were a startling white. "Or are you staying to pray?"

"I don't pray." Sean got up, buttoning his coat.

"Ha! Appropriately, you too are a heathen!" He grinned.

They slowly made their way out of the church.

"What do you mean?"

"At first, I thought that it might be otherwise. You seemed interested in the music—yet you were distracted a lot of the time. I noticed you checked your phone. I hoped you are all right. That is all."

Sean remained silent. The two men found themselves standing outside. Their breath was visible in the night air. Sean pushed his hands deeper into his pockets.

"Ah, I apologise," the other man said. "We are strangers, and I am speaking as I think you say 'out of turn'. I can tell of course that you are a visitor, although your German is truly fine! But I asked you in all concern. We are supposed to have goodwill to our fellow men at this time, not so?"

Had there been a faint emphasis on fellow *men*?

"Please forgive me, I did not mean to be rude," Sean said. He introduced himself and held out his hand. "Oh—I live here now. In Berlin."

A Flowering Wound

The other man's handshake was firm and warm. "My name is Heine."

He gave no indication whether it was his first name or surname. Although older Germans would usually introduce themselves with their surname, younger ones were much more informal, going to first-name terms immediately. Sean was completely uncertain as to Heine's age. His gravitas, his combination of formal and informal clothing made him feel that he was in the presence of someone older; but Heine's face was youthful.

"I referred to you as being a heathen. I was making a joke. You seemed distracted. You kept checking your phone."

"Did I disturb you? Sorry if I did."

"No, no, I was fine, but I was making a reference to the music. There were several versions or variations of 'Nun komm, der Heiden Heiland'. It is one of our great Advent hymns. That Buxtehude setting was most beautiful. And Johann Sebastian Bach wrote cantatas using it."

Sean laughed. "Of course. 'Come now, saviour of the heathen'. I must've heard it some time. Sometimes I think that maybe a saviour would be nice."

"Ah, I did wonder what you were needing. I could tell. Now, a drink?" Heine said. "Please, come, let us find you somewhere warm."

While they had been standing talking, it had begun to snow.

It was cold in the bedroom. Eyes still closed, Sean stretched and reached out. The sheets and duvet held warmth, but Kai was not there. Sean rolled over, then opened his eyes. The room was white, empty: the sky another sheet pinned up outside the window. Kai was in Stuttgart; it was Heine who was not there.

Heine had taken Sean to a bar in the Nikolaiviertel. Sean had found himself checking his phone again, and then telling Heine about Kai. Heine had playfully hinted at Sean's apparent desire for someone to save and console him.

"I'm not religious," Sean had said.

"I did not mean that."

"What did you mean?" But he knew.

Heine had never precisely answered any of Sean's questions. Eventually they decided to walk back to Sean's apartment. Shortly after they had set out from the bar, Sean slipped on a patch of ice. Heine had steadied him and put his arm through his. After that, he strode with confidence. As they walked, the snow swirled around them but would not settle on them. The temperature of the air kept dropping, but the snow melted on Heine's overcoat and hat. Sean felt comfortable and warm.

When they reached Strausberger Platz, Sean realised that he had not checked his phone since leaving the bar. Heine grinned as they stopped outside the entrance to Sean's block. Snowflakes quivered and flickered in the glow of the streetlights and slowly moving cars. The building reared up in front of them, an intricate glowing cliff of masonry. Heine's overcoat was damp with melted snow. Sean shivered when they unlinked arms.

Lying huddled in bed Sean wondered if he would see Heine again. He tried to corral and absorb the fading warmth where Heine had been. Perhaps he had been a victim of a charismatic, well-dressed trickster—perhaps even now his bank account was empty and his identity had been stolen. Peeping cautiously out from the duvet, Sean could see his clothes piled on the chair, and his wallet and phone on the table, seemingly undisturbed. No, he was sure that Heine had been genuine—he had understood that Sean had been alone and longing for his lover, and had given him some help. Yes, it was that time of year.

A Flowering Wound

Sean remembered how warm Heine's body had been. It was no wonder that Heine, naked, had been so taut, beautiful. Sean hugged himself as he thought of it. He wanted to stay enveloped within Heine's radiated heat: then he could forget the freezing city and stop thinking about Kai. Then he realised that was his first thought of Kai since the moment he had woken up and found himself alone.

He got dressed quickly and checked that the apartment was as empty as it felt. There was no fantasy Heine in the kitchen, preparing breakfast. Over coffee Sean checked his phone. There was nothing from Kai, but a message from Heine appeared as he was looking at the screen. It read 'Nun komm'. Now come. He smiled, and called the number. It was not recognised.

There was shopping to be done: food for the holidays. Sean had been expecting to go to the supermarket in the Ring-Center with Kai, and they would have filled a trolley with all the seasonal delicacies, wine and spirits that men of their age should avoid. Now he decided to buy as much as he could carry home. Perhaps Heine would like to come and share some of the food and drink, if Kai wasn't going to be there.

The snow had stopped during the night, but the day was grey and freezing. Nevertheless, Sean wanted to walk to the shopping centre, a mile or so further out along the boulevard beyond the domed salt-cellar towers of the Frankfurter Tor. The pavements were being cleared, and more grit and salt scattered. The street was a beige groove through the city. From his reading of Berlin history he knew that Karl-Marx-Allee had been cut through the ruins of neighbourhoods devastated by Allied air raids and the shelling by Soviet forces as they fought their way through to the centre of the city. What had risen from the pulverised desolation had been intended to symbolise the new order—a cool, rational

We, the Rescued

future to replace the outmoded chaos, errors, and passions of a past that had been brought down and consumed by fire.

As he trudged along, Sean's breath condensed as faint mist, constantly left behind and always replenished. The buildings lining the street wavered. The long façades with their ranks of windows and ornamented parapets—all edges became hazy as they fused with the grey vault of sky. He shook his head and the great blocks solidified. He was feeling warm now. It was as if losing himself in thought could create heat, or link to a reservoir of warmth.

Sitting in the U-Bahn train coming back, Sean almost missed his station. He had become absorbed in watching the ceiling of the carriage expand into the tunnel and out to the road above. Everything was grey, with a flickering as of flames leaping on the other side of a translucent barrier. His coat was becoming uncomfortable. He felt sweat trickling down between his shoulders, but couldn't rub it away without letting go of his shopping bags. He hurried onto the station platform and put his bags down. His t-shirt and shirt felt damp against his skin. He shrugged his shoulders several times, running a hand around his collar. The prickling sensation went away, but he still felt warm—even feverish.

In the bedroom he stripped off his clothes. He could feel waves of heat radiating from his body and into the chilly air of the apartment. His t-shirt was damp in places, as if he'd been running on a hot day. His shirt and jeans, dropped on the floor in a casual human shape, made him think of Kai—and Heine.

He remembered Heine's text message. Was he to go to see Heine? But he didn't know where Heine lived. He would have to settle down to wait, just as he had to for Kai. Sean wished he could make some decisions instead of having to depend on others. Dressed only in fresh t-shirt

A Flowering Wound

and jeans, Sean padded around the apartment. He was still comfortably warm, even though it was icy outside and he was dressed more for summer than winter.

The notebooks nestling against his laptop reminded him that he had work to do. He had been asked to provide a basic description and commentary to accompany an illustrated book on Berlin's post-war housing, and the associated rival ideologies between East and West. He had already made notes on the Karl-Marx-Allee development, but had still to visit its Western equivalent, the Hansaviertel. Outside, the day was brightening. The sun was successfully beginning to pierce the gloom. If anything it would get colder, but the prospect of sunlight—even low winter sunlight, weak and fleeting—would be welcome.

Sean knew that the Hansaviertel district had been so severely damaged by air raids that the decision had been made to radically rebuild it, rather than reconstruct from the ruins. The remains of houses, apartment blocks, shops, and even most of the original street plan had been swept away, replaced with a mixture of tall modernist blocks and groups of smaller, lower housing units. Each block was designed by a different architect. The buildings were set out amid open areas of grass and trees, which had in effect been turned into a continuation of the nearby Tiergarten. The intention had been to create the impression of individual buildings casually placed in a garden environment on a human scale. This was intended to contrast with the Karl-Marx-Allee development, which was a thoroughly urban conception: a street overwhelming in appearance and sometimes intimidating in scale.

Lowering grey cloud still closed the sky, but it was thinning, growing lighter from above. Bare trees studded the pale grass. Shallow drifts of snow had survived from the previous night. Frost covered the pavement. Apartment

We, the Rescued

blocks climbed above the trees, as cold and grey as the sky. Sean still felt warm, much warmer than he would have expected to. As he walked along the Händelallee, a wave of heat blew over him, as if a tremendous oven door had been opened. Then it passed. Sean staggered for a moment. He pulled off his cap, trying to let the cold air get to his head. The open cylindrical tower of the Kaiser Friedrich Memorial Church rose up ahead: there should be a bench for him to sit down.

He had read that the old gothic church had been burnt-out during the air raids, and the ruins cleared as part of the district's rebuilding. As he rested, he thought he could smell smoke, but there was no sign of fire. He wiped his forehead. He felt cooler now, but he imagined that he could take his coat off and still not be cold—unlike the passers-by, bundled-up in thick jackets and scarves. He breathed in, and the smell of smoke drifted into his nostrils. There was still no sign of anything burning. Then he became aware of a flickering. It was as if the scene, with its graded shades of grey and green, was an old film projected in front of him. He blinked. The flickering continued for a few more seconds, then faded away. He wondered if he were ill—having some sort of seizure or a heart attack. He pulled out his phone, ready to call the emergency number. There had been nothing from Kai. He read Heine's text message again.

There was a voice in his ear, but he had not made or answered a call. "Oh, when I looked back, the Händelallee was all in flames, in flames . . . "

Not long ago he thought he had friends whom he could call if he were taken ill, who would look after him and smooth things out.

Sean swallowed, and called Kai. He resigned himself to leaving another voicemail message, but to his surprise, Kai answered.

126

A Flowering Wound

"Listen, it is not a good time," Kai said, before Sean could say anything.

"Love, I just—"

"We speak soon, okay, Sean. I will send a message to you." Kai ended the call.

Sean smelled burning, but there was nothing in the air. He took deep breaths several times, ignoring the smoke he could be swallowing. He remembered childhood bonfires, the sharp taint of matches being struck and extinguished. He sighed and slipped the phone back into his pocket, but there was still a voice: "The Händelallee was in flames, in flames . . . " Then the voice stopped and the flickering ceased. He felt much better. It was as if he'd summoned Kai, whose momentary intrusion had then driven away whatever was happening to him.

On the train back to Alexanderplatz Sean felt calmer. He had wasted the first part of the afternoon. He must be coming down with some illness. He decided to go to bed as soon as he got home. In the station the steps and tunnels leading down to the U-Bahn platform were crowded. Sean let himself be carried along. He smelled smoke again, and the lights dimmed. The faces of the people round him turned grey and blurry, as if covered in ash and bandages. Was there a fire? But there was no sign of panic around him: people were moving normally, streaming towards their destinations. Colours resolved on the platform. Posters were bright and garish, and the lights glared down on the cleaned and restored tiled walls.

Sean threw his clothes into the basket and opened his wardrobe to find clean sleeping clothes. He stared at the shirts and trousers hanging in front of him: he had opened Kai's wardrobe. His clothes swayed gently like shed skins, many-textured and multi-coloured: which were real, and whose? He climbed into their bed, curling up in the duvet.

He left his phone on the table. He had opened the bedroom window, and could feel the cold twilight air entering the room, but it did not touch him. His own skin was warm. Now his body was radiating heat, just as Heine's had. Now that he was in bed, he felt fine—there were no hallucinations or sounds. He smelled the clean sheets and duvet cover, mixed faintly with the underlying astringent scent of his own sweat.

When he woke, it was still early evening, and dark outside. The air in the bedroom was glacial, but he was warm and relaxed: refreshed. He got dressed and tidied the apartment, and decided to go out for a meal. His phone showed a new message: from Kai. He knew what it would say. As he wiped his eyes he told himself that it had come as no surprise—and anyway, there was still some hope. Spending Christmas apart did not necessarily mean a split. He told himself he should have known better than to fall for a married man, but things had been different in the summer city. He lay back on the bed, wanting to wrap himself around Kai, to hold the solid grace of his body, to cradle his warmth and energy. To feel himself held in return, explored and enjoyed.

But he was hungry and thirsty. He went out.

More snow had fallen while he had been asleep, a layer as thin as dust. He walked rapidly, heading towards Alexanderplatz. He decided to find a restaurant in one of the old and narrow streets beyond the great open space of the square. The white buildings of the boulevard were smeared with glowing windows and reflected streetlights. As he walked along, he felt he was moving through years rather than metres—as if each doorway was a wasted opportunity falling behind him, never to be recovered.

He found a pleasant place to eat near Auguststrasse. It was a small, compact restaurant, but he was able to keep to

A Flowering Wound

himself and sip his beer without being noticed. The other diners were complaining about the cold weather and the icy pavements, but Sean had not been aware of any of it. He had walked rapidly and never slipped, and at some point he had pulled off his cap, as he had felt hot.

Trams ran in this part of the city. Still feeling relaxed, Sean wove his way towards the Hackescher Markt, where he knew he could catch a tram for the last part of its route towards the river, close to the museums. Drifting flakes of snow gave the city the appearance of a film set, a scene pained on glass. Everything was grey and yellow cardboard. He considered replying to Kai's message, but decided not to.

A tram was preparing to pull away—but its route was in the opposite direction to where Sean wanted to go, back through the streets behind him, up into Prenzlauer Berg and out, on through Weissensee. A man darted across the street, almost tripping over the kerb as he leapt for the closing door of the tram. Another man, standing in the doorway, reached out and helped to pull him in. The door slid shut and the tram glided away. Sean stood still, gazing at the lights of the departing tram. He could not be certain—it had all happened suddenly, and the snow and harsh streetlights could have played tricks. But he thought the man on the tram had been Heine. As he sat on the tram heading towards Georgenstrasse, he hoped that Heine would contact him again. There was a lot he would like to discuss with him—and he hoped that, as before, Heine would do more than just listen.

The day before Christmas Eve Sean bought his presents. He had long made up his mind what he would buy for Kai, and he went ahead. He found small things for Matthias and Peter, to give them when they returned from their holiday. And then he remembered the owner of the pension he had stayed at several times, while on holiday in Berlin. They had kept in touch, and Sean had a standing invitation for coffee and cake or a drink. The pension was in Weissensee, on a street that ran parallel to the tram route. He bought a bottle of the schnapps the old man liked, and decided to visit him on Christmas Eve.

During the evening Sean worked on his notes for the Hansaviertel photographs. He pushed away the experiences he had had while there. He still felt well, but something had happened to him—and more than once. He was warm, despite the freezing temperature outside. He hadn't needed to switch on the heating in the apartment. His body must be playing tricks on him. He put it down to advancing middle age—and the strain and his worrying about Kai.

He woke, still feeling clear-headed—but he knew he had dreamed. His visions had moved from day to night. He had been sitting at home while the walls flickered and flamed around him, and he heard shouts and screams and the crash of tumbling masonry. The prostrate city was being pounded from the air and from the heights to the east, and it was being consumed by fire. The flames were constrained by a transparent barrier: he was unscathed by the blazing, roaring vortices, the heat that burned brick and stone, melted metal and glass—and consumed all traces of human beings. In the dream he was sometimes uncomfortably warm, but on his side of the barrier he was safe. He put out his hand, and felt nothing but air.

Herr Kretschmar was pleased to see Sean, and immediately opened the bottle of schnapps he had brought.

"Ha, your health! Young man, I am pleased that you have stayed in Berlin." They talked for a few minutes. Then Herr Kretschmar pointed to the Berlin newspaper he had been reading. "Have you seen this? It's terrible—just along the street. What is this place coming to? And so near to Christmas."

A Flowering Wound

Sean picked up the paper and began to read where the old man indicated. A death had been reported the previous day: a man found seemingly frozen to death in Weissensee Park, close to the bathing area by the lake. The cause of death was considered uncertain because, although the man had been discovered after a very cold night, his body showed no signs of hypothermia or any other expected symptoms. A heart attack had not been ruled out. Late in the evening the man had been seen near the Hackescher Markt, but his movements after that could not be certain.

"Ach, the poor man's family," Herr Kretschmar muttered.

Sean walked on up the street towards Weissensee Park. A sharp breeze blew grit and flakes of snow into his eyes. In Antonplatz a tram from the centre of the city slowed to a stop. Among the disembarking passengers was Heine. Sean suppressed an impulse to run to him, but followed him instead, remaining at a distance. The afternoon had grown gloomy, and flurries of snow briefly obscured him. Sean lost sight of Heine in one of the long straight streets leading off Berliner Allee near the park.

Snow was falling heavily by the time Sean reached home. Walls glittered with frost. The pavement in front of his block had been swept clean, but it could not remain so for long. In the apartment he felt the cold filter down onto him. He switched on the heating and drew the blinds, making sure all windows were firmly closed. He cooked a meal and opened a bottle of wine, and settled down on the sofa. Perhaps Kai would change his mind and come back after all—maybe his wife would release him. They should have been exchanging their presents, drinking wine together, and perhaps listening to the carols from King's College.

It was very quiet in the flat. He tried to read, but there was no concentration. He looked around at the pale walls, the pools of soft light from the lamps, the shadows. He shivered. He could hardly believe that he had spent much of the last few days feeling hot and feverish.

His phone remained inert, its screen black, unfathomable. It was warm in the room, but he still felt cold. He made coffee, but he shivered as he drank it. He longed for the summer, for the city Berlin had been as it shimmered and drowsed in the sunlight of that last August and September. Then he had been consumed by heat, and had welcomed it and embraced it. More than ever he ached for it now.

Kai's phone number was not recognised. Heine's was still unrecognised. Only his message remained: Come, now. Sean yearned to go.

His phone woke him. The bedroom was full of cold blue light: the sky was clear and deep. The text message was from Heine.

He was waiting outside, at the top of the steps leading down to the U-Bahn station. He seemed unaffected by the cold. Sean wanted to hug him, but they shook hands, as if they had been work colleagues giving each other the standard Christmas greetings. Warmth flowed into Sean.

"I'm so pleased to see you again," Sean said. "I wondered if I ever would."

Heine smiled. "Let us go home, Sean. Come."

"Home? Back to your place? Weissensee—"

He nodded. "Yes. Oh, and I did see you."

When they were sitting together in the tram, Sean said, "I never told Kai about you. He never gave me the chance, but I would've done."

Much of the snow that had fallen during the night still remained untouched, hard and frozen. The low sun had not yet melted any frost. Once, Sean looked back along the street. Heine's footprints were clear, as if melted into the snow and frost. None of the other few pedestrians seemed to notice.

A Flowering Wound

They paused outside a house, set back in a garden, behind a crumbling wall. Heine produced a key.

"May I stay all day?" Sean asked.

Heine smiled. To Sean it was perfection. Now he was glad that Kai had made his choice.

"Come in," Heine said.

The afternoon waned. Heine got up to go around the house switching on lights and drawing curtains. Sean had long since stopped shivering.

"I dream of heat, I long for it," Sean whispered. "Even though I don't feel it, I'm burning. I want to burn. That's all I want now. Please, Heine. Please."

The Man Ahead

They arrive at the square a few minutes past noon. People stroll around in island clusters. A group of drummers set up their equipment in the bandstand. Ryan walks just behind Simon and Chris, looking around at the activity. He checks his phone, but there are no new emails or missed messages.

"Are you okay?" Simon asks. His brow furrows as he puts on a pair of sunglasses. "Not tired?"

Ryan shakes his head. "I'm fine. Just getting a bit hot in the sun. The walk here, taking all those photos."

Chris walks on ahead and stands by an empty bench.

"We can sit down," Simon says. "We'll still be in the sun for a bit, but we can relax before the march." He fingers the whistle hanging on its lanyard around his neck. Ryan has one too, passed on by Chris after Simon had bought it for him. Ryan is sure Simon didn't see that he caught the expression on his face. He loathes whistles, and doesn't intend to use his.

"Okay." They walk towards the bench. Chris's thumbs are already flying across the smooth face of his phone. His rainbow wristband glows against reddening skin. "I'm going to buy one of those wristbands," Ryan says. "I saw a stall back there."

Simon holds out his hand. "I'll look after your food and water."

"Thanks." Ryan hands over the lunch he bought earlier but keeps the bottle of water.

A Flowering Wound

He feels self-conscious, out of place, but is glad to be where he is: in this city, in the square, in the sun, seeing Simon again. It was Simon who invited him to stay, saying he would be welcome to come for a few days, and that Chris was looking forward to meeting him at last. They were going to attend the city's annual Pride celebration, and thought that Ryan would enjoy it. He might meet someone . . .

Slipping the coloured band onto his wrist, Ryan wanders on, past the row of stalls. The atmosphere is friendly, relaxed. Everyone seems to know everyone else. Simon and Chris come back into view. Chris sits towards the centre of the bench, staring at his phone, with Simon to his left, which manoeuvres Ryan into the space between Simon and the end of the bench. The only man he knows is Simon—Chris materialised later, through scrawled notes in the Christmas and birthday cards Simon had never ceased to send. One sender became two, emphasising to Ryan his continuing aloneness.

Now, as he sees how Simon and Chris have placed themselves, he begins to reflect who out of the three of them might really be the most alone. Perhaps he made a mistake in agreeing to visit his friend, to see him again after all this time. He pushes away the uncertainty by uncapping his bottle of water and taking a drink. The clear plastic is still cold enough to be covered in condensation, and he rubs the bottle against his forehead. The sun throbs as insistently as the drummers. Ryan is sure his neck and shoulders are already beginning to burn. He should have brought a hat with him.

Walking up to the bench Ryan hears Chris muttering to Simon. His tone doesn't sound too friendly. The drummers' beat thumps from the loudspeakers. Ryan decides to take more time, walk on past, and head back towards the stalls. But Simon sees him and waves. Then he turns towards

The Man Ahead

Chris, their heads moving close in. Perhaps they're not talking about him after all. Why should they?

Ryan sits down. Simon gives him his food and touches his new wristband. "Maybe I should get a new one, too," he says. "Mine is last year's!"

Chris's phone bawls out its tune, swiftly cut off as he stands up to answer. "Yeah . . . No . . . Yeah . . . " Ryan looks down at the worn paving slab between his feet. Simon is checking for messages. His own phone remains inert.

As the bench fills, Ryan is pushed up against the grey wooden arm. Its harsh grainy texture imprints itself on his skin. Simon's leg presses against his. "They said to bring sun cream," a voice calls out from the other end of the bench. "I said they did." The sun rinses all colour out of the sky, and turns City Hall and the other bulky buildings surrounding the square into mere tinted shapes. Beige stone and pale red brick recycle the sunlight. There is no shade in this part of the square.

Simon's arms burn, just as Ryan's are. Soon Simon's arms will be as red as the bricks of the wall behind them. He remembers Simon hugging him, years ago: the strength in those arms. There are still times when he wishes he had tried to explain how he really felt—but then, he had been so sure that the decade separating him from Simon would be unbridgeable. Ryan hadn't wanted to be the one to fall, or have to watch Simon tumble away, out of his sight. Their friendship had remained just that, ever since.

Ryan looks up at the sun—as if, during the moment he can bear to, it would flood into his eyes, wash through him, and scour out thoughts he would rather not entertain. There was, there is, no point in thinking. Simon is with Chris, and he is on his own again. He screws his eyes shut, but still gazes up into the empty sky. Heat pounds his face. Ghostly electric suns float across a red background.

136

A Flowering Wound

Someone's drawling loudly into his phone. "Right, yeah, it *is* hot. What? No, he doesn't." Ryan opens his eyes and realises it's still Chris. Simon turns to him, smiling as he shields his eyes. "He's talking to Karl. You met him last night, just before we had to go. Short black hair, tanned, tattoo, nice definition. Tall, but not quite as tall as Chris. Or were you thinking about someone else, eh Ryan?"

"You've described just about everyone I met last night," Ryan says, returning Simon's smile. "Okay, no, not exactly." He remembers how he used to joke that Simon was in good shape for his age; and it was true—still is. He wishes Simon would smile and laugh more—and not just when with an old friend.

"Karl's here in the city centre, but doesn't want to go on the march. Surprise, surprise, he's having a few drinks. He wants Chris to meet up with him, keep him company. Chris said he probably will, just for a few minutes."

"During the march?"

"Well . . . Yes, maybe. I told Chris it'd be good if we could all walk together. It's only a few hundred yards, around the square and to the front of the Cathedral and back again. But it might just be you and me, for some of it, anyway."

Simon turns away again, his smile just a little too quick to wipe itself from his face.

A voice flares from the loudspeaker. Ryan leans forward to hear, but the words are distorted, as empty of content as the sky and square are of detail and depth. "We're starting off in about five minutes," Simon says. "When the City Hall clock chimes the hour and they start to ring the Cathedral bells." A shadow falls across them, before sliding away. Chris looks down on Simon and says something Ryan can't hear. He pulls on his baseball cap, slips his phone into the pocket of his shorts. Simon nods.

The Man Ahead

"Karl's by Cathedral Gate," Simon says. "Chris is going straight there and he'll join the march when we reach them."

"Okay," Ryan says.

"Hey, it's all right, Ryan," Simon says. "You know Chris—well, no, you don't, really, do you? Not yet, anyway."

Rainbow flags and banners flop listlessly in the cloying air. High above them a bell starts to toll, its clangour falling into the square, echoing around the buildings and reverberating through the crowd. A distant peal of bells answers. Cheering breaks out, with a renewed burst of drumming from the loudspeakers.

"You ready?" Simon says, lightly touching Ryan's thigh as he gets up. "All okay for water and food?" Ryan nods and swallows more water. He picks up his bag of sandwiches and crisps. Ryan loves Simon's simple concern and kindness. "Simon's a really nice guy," he remembers being told, over and over again, by everyone. "He'll put himself out for you." Being together could have so easily become a constant surrender to it—a voluntary forgetting, in acceptance for which there would never be a price formally proposed, except what he wished to pay. Another reason not to have started out across the bridge . . . Ryan wonders how it works for Chris, or even if he lets it. "We should've brought hats," Simon says, grinning.

Ryan finds himself sandwiched with Simon between a group of women draped in flowing green robes and a line of men wearing a uniform he doesn't quite recognise. Simon stops for a moment to shake hands with two of the men. Ryan walks backwards for two or three steps, making sure he stays ahead so Simon can see him to walk beside him again. "Police," Simon tells him, "believe it or not. Or the support guys, rather." Two of the women just ahead of them are carrying a banner, but Ryan can't make out the lettering or the symbol in the centre. It's almost painful to look up

A Flowering Wound

and try to decipher them: there's too much light and heat waiting to drown him.

Shoppers stand on the pavement as the march goes past. Some are clearly supportive, while others have stopped to look on with bemusement, shading their eyes. There seems to be no hostility. The marchers turn into a narrow street which is closed to traffic. At last they are in shadow: the sky is reduced to a bleached strip directly overhead.

"We'll be a bit cooler for a few minutes," Simon says, looking around him. Ryan smiles and drinks some water.

"You okay, Ryan?"

"Yeah, I'm enjoying it. I need to get out more."

Simon giggles. "Any time," he says.

"You might meet someone," Simon had said. Then Ryan remembers that Simon hadn't said it—he had thought it for himself, imagined it possible. Perhaps there is still time, after all.

Ahead of them a curtain of gold severs the shadow-filled street. They approach a crossroads, where the sun reasserts itself. "All these streets are closed for the day, or were pedestrianised anyway," Simon says. "We should see Chris in a minute."

To his right Ryan sees a half-timbered building festooned with rainbow flags. Men stand on the pavement, holding drinks and chatting into phones. Several hold up their phones and take photographs. There is an outbreak of cheering and clapping as people step into the road and join the march. Over the door the pub's name is still visible: The City Vaults. He remembers it's one of the places Simon and Chris go to—the previous night Simon talked about going there, but they hadn't made it that far. They had taken Ryan to the King's Head, where they had stayed. Chris had seemed to spend most of the evening texting and vanishing for cigarettes, leaving Simon free to talk. When friends came over, he introduced Ryan and tried to make sure he was included in the conversation. As they walked home, Simon had turned to Chris and said, "Adam showed up. I think he really liked Ryan. We could ask him to dinner before Ryan goes back home. What do you think?" Chris tapped at his phone and brushed his fingers across its screen. "Yeah, if you like."

"No, it doesn't matter, it's okay," Ryan says.

"What's that?" Simon asks.

Ryan stumbles into the heat of the crossroads. He wants to go back into the calming shadow or rush on ahead to where it starts again. "Oh, nothing," he replies. "I got thinking for a moment. Always dangerous for me, eh?"

"Don't put yourself down, Ryan."

In the shade once more, whistles shrill off the old buildings. The police support officers fall further behind, replaced by a group of four or five young men, constantly milling around and keeping pace with each other, but otherwise having no apparent connection. A boy wearing a plain white T shirt and cut-off black jeans brushes a wing of blond hair out of his eyes and waves. Ryan hesitates, then waves back.

Ryan glimpses Karl: one of the tanned men standing outside the pub talking at his phone. But he can't be entirely sure it is him. The man hurries off in the direction of the march, as if aiming to outrun it. His white and red checked shirt flickers in the crowd ahead, darting from side to side on the pavement: the same man, phone still glued to his ear. Ryan looks to see if Simon notices, but there's no sign. Simon gulps water from his bottle and wipes his eyes with the back of his hand.

Bells start to peal again, a cataract of sound crashing into the street. "Almost at Cathedral Gate," Simon says. "Then we go back to where we started by a parallel route."

"I don't see Chris yet," Ryan says. Almost immediately he wishes he hadn't said anything. Does Simon really expect

A Flowering Wound

Chris to meet him now? Surely he could work out what's happening? The phones already know; and the sky and sun see everything.

"He said he'd be around here," Simon says. "He's probably still in the pub. I'll sort it out with him when we do see him."

They walk past the gateway leading to the Cathedral Close. In the glare it is the colour of beach sand, and appears scarcely more solid. The carved gothic stonework seems about to droop, to melt down and lose all definition, smoothing out and absorbing its features. Ryan's phone chimes. He squints at the screen. The march is back in the sunshine, and he can see nothing except his own face reflected in the tiny panel of smooth, smeared glass. He holds up the phone and takes photographs as they move, not checking the resulting images.

The green-shrouded women reappear in front of them. A loudspeaker asks the crowd to wait in the square after returning there, to reassemble and listen to a speech and show their thanks to the organisers. Ryan looks around, scanning the crowd. Karl is nowhere to be seen. Then Chris is standing at the corner of the next street, cap pushed back and forehead ridged in confusion. The marchers stream past. Simon doesn't show any sign of having seen him. Ryan opens his mouth and closes it again. At the edge of his vision he sees the other man appear next to Chris. They turn away and head up the side street.

The square opens out in front of them. The City Hall rises up, filling one entire side like a beached ocean liner. Ryan still grasps his phone, but the screen is black, empty. He's not sure when he stopped taking photos. Simon catches at his wrist, hand closing around it and taking hold. He had been about to cross into the overwhelming volume of scorching heat and light.

The Man Ahead

"Let's wait here a second," Simon says. They stand back, letting people walk on past them. Ryan drinks the rest of his water. "Are you hungry yet, Ryan? In a minute we can go to the park or sit by the river, if you like. It'll be quieter there, and we can eat our lunch. We can get some more water as well."

When had Simon's "we" come to seem to mean two rather than three? Ryan shuffles possibilities like playing cards. No, surely he meant to include Chris as well. He presses a button and stares at his phone, but still can't read the screen. He can't think of anyone else except Simon who would have sent him a text; he didn't remember giving Adam his number.

"I've finished my water," Ryan says, stuffing the bottle into a bin. The black plastic bag crackles. "I'll buy some more later."

Simon looks at his watch. Applause drifts out of the square, and over them. "Pity Chris didn't make it," he murmurs. "I've caught sight of Karl enough times, but not Chris." He stops a group of young men as they walk past and asks to photograph them. They pose and smile, pulling faces and laughing.

"Let's go to the park," Simon says. "We can sit under the trees. I'm getting hungry now. Would you like to have a pizza or something in the city centre later? We could go to the King's Head again afterwards, perhaps. It'll be really nice in the garden out back. There'll be more friends there."

Ryan finishes his sandwich. Simon gets up. "Here, give me your rubbish. I'll throw it away with mine. Do you want to get anything else?"

He shakes his head and takes out his phone. The screen bursts into life, easily readable now, in the shade of the trees. He can't find a text message. He's sure he didn't delete it by mistake. Maybe it had been someone else's phone

A Flowering Wound

all along. He checks again. No missed calls, either. Ryan quickly scrolls through his photos. Most of them seem to be far too bright, sun-bleached, capturing no more than indistinct forms and profiles of heads and bodies.

They remain in the park, talking. Every few minutes Simon checks his phone, sometimes smiling as he sends a message or update. Later they walk back through the city centre and down to the river. Whenever Ryan glimpses the spire of the Cathedral, it seems ready to leap at the sky, a dart to pierce it, to break through.

Eventually Ryan has to ask: "Have you heard from Chris? I've been looking out, but—I'm pretty sure I haven't seen him."

"No, nothing. I phoned home and there was no answer. And I left a message on his phone. I don't suppose anything could have happened. Not that I can think of. Anyway, Karl will look after him."

Back at Simon's there's no sign of Chris. Ryan hadn't taken much notice of what seemed to belong to whom, but now nothing seems out of place or missing. There are no gaps. He sits down on the sofa while Simon goes to the kitchen to make coffee. Soft light from the lamp standing on a small table paints the umber walls. The window is a black square. Ryan walks through to the bathroom to wash his face. The flannel he'd crammed into his wash bag that morning is still damp; the others, hanging on chrome-plated hooks next to the basin, are bone dry.

Simon says, "I've made the coffee strong. See, I remembered that's how you like it, as I do. And no milk, no sugar—that's right, isn't it." Ryan had only drunk orange juice at breakfast. "Are you feeling tired?"

He sips the scalding coffee gratefully. "Yeah, a bit. Maybe I shouldn't have had that last pint. I feel okay, though. The walk home was good. It's a lovely night."

The Man Ahead

"You're fine," Simon says, getting up. "Well, I'm going to bed. Stay up as long as you like. Get up when you want. You know where everything is." He pats Ryan on the head, playfully sliding his hand lightly down the curve of his neck to rest on his shoulder. Then he says, "Sleep well, Ryan."

Ryan switches off all but one of the lamps and stands at the window, sipping his coffee. In the distance the spire of the Cathedral, now floodlit, jabs at the night. Other windows wink at him, shining out from behind the barely moving trees.

Once in bed, Ryan is wide awake. In the street a car door slams. The afternoon's events replay in his mind: the walk around the city centre with Simon and Chris, arriving at the square in front of City Hall, going on the march. He pushes the duvet back.

His upper body prickles with heat. The cream and terra-cotta buildings grow pale. Rainbow flags and bunting taunt the washed-out sky. The narrow street begins to widen as the marchers draw closer to the square. There are not as many people around him as there should be. But if he remembers more, they have withdrawn, one by one, absorbed into transparency.

It's been a while since he last saw Karl. And Simon hasn't mentioned Chris for a long time. Ahead of them the ranked windows of City Hall and the other public buildings flash in the sun. Heat pours off brickwork and stone, metal and glass. He savours the cool marble of the long, empty corridors inside.

Ryan sees Chris, standing by himself. Ryan clutches at Simon's hand, to let him know. Simon takes no notice. Both men continue walking. Chris seems to be alone. Marchers fade out around him, oblivious. Chris looks around, shading his eyes against the glare, as if searching for a face—anybody, anything—he might know. He still grips his phone.

A Flowering Wound

"It's Chris. He's over there!" Ryan says, but Simon doesn't acknowledge him. Chris raises the phone to his ear. He is mouthing Simon's name, a series of invocations. Ryan cannot speak. Chris crosses to the paved central area of the square, looking at each of the diminishing number of people he passes. Bright t-shirts and rainbow lanyards lose their colours; tanned skin fades through pink to doughy white and passes into plain air. Shadows evaporate.

Chris walks on, towards the middle of the square. The buildings lining the square flare up and ebb away into the hot sunlight. There is nobody else anywhere near him now.

Someone squeezes Ryan's shoulder, and shakes him, gently but insistently. He doesn't want to lose sight of Chris, as Simon still shows no interest at all. Simon grins and laughs, holding out Ryan's phone. "Didn't mean to startle you," he says. "I hope it was a pleasant dream!" The bedroom window is open, letting in the cool morning air. "You left your phone on the sofa last night. I heard it go when I was making the coffee. You gave Adam your number, didn't you?"

Simon and Ryan hug each other again just before Ryan boards his coach. "You're welcome anytime," Simon says. "Come again. Don't forget. Let's not leave it so long." They smile and wave as the coach reverses out and pulls away. It's still hot outside. The streets are busy and the pavements crowded. Shopping parades glide past the window. His phone chimes, and he reads Simon's message thanking him again. He reaches for his sunglasses. Traffic lights blink and the coach accelerates. As the air conditioning starts up, Ryan settles back and closes his eyes. The low-level purr soon becomes inaudible.

Once more the tall figure approaches out of the haze. His eyes dart from side to side, desperately searching the vast space. He looks around, his face betraying increasing

The Man Ahead

anxiety and dismay; yet in his disappointment still sustained by hope. Chris aches for someone to find and comfort him—for the sound, at last, of the one familiar voice he longs to hear, calling out his name and inviting him to come back home. Alone in the silent and empty square, he hesitates before walking on, dwindling as distance takes him, blurring into the heat.

Somewhere, a man is crying for his friend.

Twilight of the Airships

The new exhibition in the display window of Gabriel Lereanu's shop was colourful and impressive. Lereanu had calculated that it would cause passersby to stop and stare, and entice many who stopped and stared into entering his shop and to make a purchase. Lereanu's business sense was acute and had rarely let him down. On this occasion, too, it had worked.

Gabriel Lereanu owned a stamp and coin shop in Sinaia Boulevard—the broad, curving street sliced through Steaua de Munte's Old Town at the end of the nineteenth century and lined with elegant apartments and shops, large and small. Lereanu was always careful to ensure that the displays in the windows of his shop were in keeping with the smart surroundings. Behind the specially toughened glass Lereanu would lay out his merchandise. Low down, at the front, where children could easily see them, were sets of gaudy postage stamps from obscure countries with low rates of literacy and high turnovers in presidents. Further back and higher up were displays of single stamps and coins, rare pieces carefully placed and labelled. Sometimes Lereanu also displayed a range of collectable banknotes or the share certificates of long-vanished corporations whose taste in flamboyant or elegant design had been more certain than their success in commerce.

It was not only in Steaua de Munte that Lereanu and his business was known. He had spent years giving painstaking attention to prudent advertising in specialist journals and the circulation of catalogues restricted to a slowly growing clientele. He had worked hard at growing his reputation for knowledge, probity, and the ability to supply his customers' requirements, no matter how scarce and unusual. And his satisfied customers spread the word about the exemplary service they had received. All this ensured that Lereanu never needed to actually display the choicest, the most intriguing, and the most remarkable—let alone the most valuable—of the items that he had in stock to sell. Buyers and vendors alike beat a path to his Art Nouveau door.

The motivation behind the display in Gabriel Lereanu's shop window had been provided by his son Sorin. As well as being an enthusiastic collector of stamps and associated items of postal history since childhood, the young man was also passionately interested in aviation, and particularly the great rigid dirigible airships developed since the turn of the century by Count Ferdinand von Zeppelin and his successors and competitors. Over the years Sorin had built up a network of pen-friends of his own age and particular combination of interests. It was only rarely that the day's post did not bring him a crop of letters, postcards, and packets from Germany, the Soviet Union, the United States, and Great Britain, among others. Sorin would write back to his correspondents, discussing the latest developments and exploits in airship aviation, as well as exchanging stamps and other items with his international contacts. And the younger Lereanu had inherited his father's well-honed commercial sense. When Sorin saw the chance to make use of his two main interests, and also bring in extra income to the family business, he eagerly seized the opportunity. Sorin quickly convinced the older Lereanu that the forthcoming flight of the new German airship *Friedrich der Grosse* across

A Flowering Wound

Romania would be a major event well worth marking. The National Socialists had decided that the flight would boost their prestige, and decreed that the new airship fly over some of the countries they desired to impress. When it was revealed that its planned route across the mountains would take the enormous airship over Steaua de Munte, Gabriel Lereanu congratulated himself on having such a shrewd son and heir. A week or so later it was announced that the newest addition to the Soviet Union's fleet of airships, the *Oktober*, would also be making its longest trial flight to date at about the same time. For the Soviet Government it was an opportunity to gain some positive coverage while reminding the world of the superiority of Communism over National Socialism. The powers behind the rival ideologies found themselves with the prospect of an unexpected competition. Diplomats, politicians, and engineers conferred, and for a short time the intoxicating winds of the upper air blew through the Foreign Ministries of both countries. It was agreed that the much-vaunted new airships would be allowed to briefly share the sky over Steaua de Munte as they flew on their separate paths. And when the Lereanus heard this news, both men all but danced for joy.

Father and son stood together outside the shop and admired the bright display. Dominating the window, and providing the background, was a huge poster that Sorin had secured through his pen-friend in Leningrad. From a sea of red flags and a row of sketchily-painted but clearly cyclopean hangars the vast shape of the *Oktober* loomed out, its dark bulk seeming about to burst through into the spectator's own sky and overwhelm with its engulfing shadow. The new airship dominated its sister ships *Pravda* and *Lenin*, which were rendered miniscule by comparison. The pen-friend had assured Sorin that the text on the poster translated as *On the basis of our gigantic achievements in*

Twilight of the Airships

metal, machinery and grain, we will build giants of the air!
Our airships demonstrate great and fraternal advances!

Gabriel Lereanu could not read Russian. In order to be certain that the poster would not cause offence to the local Legionaries or anyone else, Lereanu had secured permission from the mayor to display it in his window. Lereanu hoped the notice to that effect that he placed nearby would prevent accusations of Bolshevism or any other trouble. He also reflected that the small gift that he had made to the mayor—already a regular customer—had done no harm in furthering the request. Lereanu had taken from his stock a gleaming proof specimen of the stylish silver crown coin recently struck to commemorate the Jubilee of King George V of England, and left the rest to the mayor's conscience as well as the desire to enlarge his coin collection. Lereanu still had his doubts about the poster, but its visual impact couldn't be denied. Sorin had also provided a selection of maps showing the epic inter-continental flights already undertaken by the visiting airships' sister crafts, and publicity photographs showing spectacular views from their control gondolas of rivers and wide plains, forests, mountains, and wastes of hot desert and arctic ice. There were also photos taken from the ground showing the giants' stately progresses over many of the world's greatest cities and monuments.

The two men had assembled a large and varied collection of stamps, coins and other related items for sale. There were sets of postage and airmail stamps and various special issues from numerous countries depicting airships, and a number of items of mail that had been carried on airship flights and had received commemorative stamps, postmarks, and other endorsements. There was a row of the new German silver five mark coins which featured the *Friedrich der Grosse* on the reverse. Many items featured the swastika and hammer and sickle, both now apparently as unavoidable in the air

A Flowering Wound

as on the ground. Perhaps the most poignant exhibit—and the only one not for sale—was an envelope, slightly charred around the edges, bearing a postmark commemorating the inaugural flight to India by the British airship R101. There were envelopes that had been carried on board its highly successful sister craft R100, as well as some small pieces of the outer fabric and gasbags cut from the airship and preserved before it was broken up for scrap in the aftermath of the tragedy that befell the other.

And the impending flights of the *Friedrich der Grosse* and the *Oktober* carried with them the lure and glamour of exceptionally unusual items of franked mail transported on both airships. Sorin had called in favours and made promises among his contacts in the worlds of philately and aviation. And now in the mailbags on each airship there were a large number of self-addressed letters and cards, each covered in bright newly issued commemorative postage stamps and awaiting the special postmarks and endorsements that would set the envelopes apart as items of unique importance as well as associational and monetary value.

Lereanu patted his son on the shoulder, and they went back inside the shop. During the day a constant stream of people walked along Sinaia Boulevard, and most seemed to stop outside Lereanu's shop and examine the display, if only for a few seconds. Some entered and made enquiries. In the early afternoon a well-dressed man came into the shop and quietly rebuked Lereanu for the prominence given to the Soviet poster. Lereanu thought that his critic seemed to be slightly drunk, most likely from the effects of the fine plum brandy sold in the numerous bars of the nearby Hotel Paris. And his German accent told Lereanu what to expect. But it was his policy that anyone who entered the shop was a potential customer and an opportunity for a sale, and he was listened to with courtesy. Lereanu patiently explained that

Twilight of the Airships

there were German stamps and coins on display as well, but if he could have obtained a similar poster or advertisement that extolled German airships, he would have made use of it.

"Germany and Russia are both great nations," Lereanu said. "They are forging ahead in this particular field of aviation, so my son never tires of telling me."

The German leaned across the counter and pressed Lereanu's hand. "Exactly! Mine too! How he talks! Now, I meant nothing personal with my comments. You are in business and so am I. Our countries should be closer friends. But to be here and to see those Russian symbols dominating ours . . . Listen, my dear sir, I have contacts at home and will have someone send you something suitable for your display. Do you agree?" He grabbed Lereanu's hand and shook it vigorously.

"Naturally, sir, we would be grateful if you could provide anything to enhance this place and to further the progress of friendship and trade between Germany and Romania," Lereanu replied.

"Of course you would! I fought in the East during the war. We would never have fought against Romania if we hadn't been made to. The Russians, though—"

"Yes, I fought as well," Lereanu snapped. "I don't want another war with anyone. But Russia is closer than Germany. Look at any map! And with these giant airships . . . "

"I will keep my promise and have sent to you something good for your window. Ha! One might then almost believe that the Reich and the Russians were in alliance, their magnificent craft and powerful symbols so close together! Of course, if the Leader desired and it suited the Reich we would indeed work with the Bolsheviks. But that will never happen, believe me!"

Shortly afterwards Lereanu's visitor handed over his business card and left the shop, promising again to have a poster or similar display object sent from Germany straight away. Lereanu read the business card, flicking it between his fingers before filing it away with all the others he'd kept over the years. Then he started to swear under his breath. It was unforgiveable, he thought. He'd lost his temper with a potential customer—just for a moment—and hadn't attempted to sell him a single thing.

A few days later a strong cardboard tube, well wrapped in brown paper and covered with postage stamps and customs declarations, was delivered to the shop. A label revealed that the package had been sent via the Trade Delegation of the German Embassy in Bucharest. Lereanu carefully cut away the stamps and put them to one side. He extracted a roll of shiny paper from its protective packaging and laid it out on the counter, weighting the corners down with piles of coins waiting to be sorted and graded. Lereanu's visitor had fulfilled his promise. He had had a poster sent from the German Airship Company showing its newest and largest airship, *Friedrich der Grosse*, alongside the existing *Graf Zeppelin* and *Hindenburg* and superimposed on a globe criss-crossed by the routes of their scheduled and anticipated commercial flights. The message proclaimed was that the reinvigorated German Reich was at the centre of a new world order of travel, exploration, and enterprise, and intended to use its expanding expertise in airship aviation to achieve ascendancy in the field. Lereanu telephoned for his son to come down to the shop and reorganise the display window.

❧

The day of the airships' flight over the town arrived. By then Gabriel Lereanu had sold most of the airship-related merchandise he had in stock in his shop, although with the

Twilight of the Airships

agreement of the buyers most of it had been left on display. He had firm orders for all the envelopes and cards that he and his son had arranged to be carried on the two flights and wished to sell. Sorin had decided that he would retain some of them for his own collection.

By late morning the sky had cleared, and the sun shone down out of an empty blue sky. Although it was a fine day in the middle of April, there was a brisk breeze that kept the day from getting too warm. Steaua de Munte glowed in the clear sharp sunlight. From the bare heights of Star Hill the Castle, rising from its hill on the other side of town, looked like a newly cleaned model close enough to grasp, with its white walls and towers, red roofs and soaring gothic church all gleaming in the morning light. The closely packed houses of the Old Town between them lapped at the bases of the two hills like solidified waves. On the other side of the river the New Town with its grid of squares and streets was a carpet of pastel colours laid out in the sun. Smoke pouring from the chimneys of houses and factories attempted to stain the sky, but was blown away by the steady wind. Trams glided along the growing length of University Avenue past the white cubes and colonnades of the new campus.

Sorin had written enthusiastically to his pen-friends about his family's preparations for the day and their plans for marking it. Now he walked to the railway station to meet Rainer, a fellow airship enthusiast from Berlin who was on a holiday sailing down the Danube with some of his student friends. He had sent a telegram advising that he had decided to break his journey and visit Steaua de Munte to join Sorin and see the airships with him.

Several travellers got out of the train. It was obvious to Sorin which of them was his visitor. Rainer looked just like Sorin had imagined he would: tall and very fair-haired, with

A Flowering Wound

a ruddy complexion now glowing from windburn. Rainer looked around him and then strode over to where Sorin waited and introduced himself in halting Romanian. "But we will speak German or English if that is in order," Rainer said. "I think that will be all right if you speak them as well as you write them! Sorin, I am very pleased to be here."

"Nobody seems to be as excited as we are," Sorin said, as the two men shook hands vigorously. "Everything's going on much as normal round here!"

"I don't know how the *Oktober* is doing, but *Grosser Fritz* still isn't due until about sunset, right?"

Sorin laughed. "*Big Fritz*. I like that. I bet you have to keep quiet about that nickname, though, eh? I think your leaders can be rather serious about such things, can't they?"

Rainer grinned. "Yes, sometimes, but we are not all like that. They say that in 1933 Dr. Eckener told Hitler where to get off, and he still tells Goebbels what he can do with his propaganda! All the same, this is a great day. When I first saw the *Graf Zeppelin* at Tempelhof, I was so proud! I really hope I can get a job with the Zeppelin Company when I finish university and get my qualifications. So far helping to clean the engine gondolas and holding onto mooring lines is the nearest I've got to actually travelling in an airship."

It had been arranged that Rainer would stay the night. As they walked away from the station, Sorin described the display in the shop window and explained how it came to feature airship posters from both Germany and the Soviet Union. "But today is all about friendly rivalry only, I hope," he added.

After lunch Sorin showed Rainer around the shop before they went up to the apartment to look at his collection of airship stamps and covers. Rainer had brought some photographs of the *Graf Zeppelin* and *Hindenburg* moored at Tempelhof. Sorin was astounded by the size of the nearly

155

Twilight of the Airships

completed airport buildings. Enormous as the airships were, they were still dwarfed by the vast sweep of the aircraft hangars curving out from either side of the massive central hall. It was as if the hangars were waiting to enfold the entire open space of the airport—including the gnat-sized aircraft on the runways and the airship floating at its mooring—in one overpowering embrace of stone and glass and metal.

Later in the afternoon Sorin and Rainer took a walk along the boulevard and around Star Square. They were dismayed to notice a layer of cloud rising up from the north, sliding across the sky like milk spilt on glass. "It was cloudy when I woke up, then it cleared," Sorin said. "If we can't get to see the airships today I don't suppose there'll ever be another opportunity. Or at least not for a very long time." Even as they watched, the clouds started darkening to a deeper grey, and an early dusk began to fall. Soon, as the breeze dropped away, it was clear that the twilight was staying.

Gabriel Lereanu had arranged to have the use of a room at the top of one of the towers of the Castle. "It'll be a long time before the mayor and I use up all the favours we owe each other!" he'd said. Two of Lereanu's friends worked in radio and possessed the apparatus that would allow them to listen in on the transmissions from both airships as they passed overhead. Between them they knew a fair amount of both German and Russian; with Rainer there as well, they expected to be able to understand most of anything that they overheard.

An hour before sunset Sorin and Rainer set out in Lereanu's car for the short journey to the Castle. Although it was a spring evening, it felt more like a late afternoon in October. The others were waiting at the foot of the wide stone stairway that coiled up around the slope of Castle Hill. Sorin hung a pair of binoculars and his camera around his neck. Rainer held a small camera as well. The two radio men

A Flowering Wound

carried the radio equipment up the shallow steps, discussing how quickly they could reassemble it at the top of the tower.

Before long, all was ready. Lereanu lit the lamps placed around the room. As Sorin and Rainer wandered from window to window, gazing down at the town spreading out from the base of Castle Hill, Lereanu helped to set up the radio receiver and connect the aerial. One of the radio men hung the aerial wire down from the railing of the small sheltered terrace that bit into one side of the tower room. Outside, the sky grew darker as evening fell. In the west the sunset was a red smear behind the cloud low on the horizon. There was no wind and no sign that the cloud would clear away.

"Is everything on schedule?" Rainer asked.

Lereanu nodded. "I got the calls just before we left home. I'd arranged to have reports phoned through from Cernăuți and Oradea when the airships were spotted there. They're just about keeping to the planned times."

"Where are they flying from?" one of the radio men asked.

"The *Oktober* is flying direct from Dolgoprudny," Sorin replied. "And I think the *Friedrich der Grosse* started out from Friedrichshafen, but flew via Berlin first."

"Yes, that is correct," Rainer added. "But are we going to get the chance to see them?"

"It doesn't look very hopeful," Lereanu said, coming in from the terrace.

"Maybe we will still be able to hear them?" Rainer said. "I don't know about the Russian airship, but the *Friedrich der Grosse* isn't silent. Airships are not really 'silent giants' at all. Those engines do make quite a bit of noise!"

The last of the sunset faded away. Shadows flowed sinuously over the walls in the cramped space. The dim room at the top of the tower was silent except for the sounds that the radio picked up out of the air. The lights of the town

Twilight of the Airships

strewn out far below shone in the gloom. A growing hush came with the night; sounds seemed to be able to rise no higher than the rooftops. The radio men kept on making adjustments to the apparatus, swearing under their breath. "Well, that's it," one of them finally said. "We should be able to hear what both crews say, as long as they pass over near where we are and use the usual frequencies. It'll be better with the headphones. You can take turns listening in."

Sorin felt his heart beginning to beat faster as the time for the airships to fly over drew steadily nearer. He imagined a silent world of moonlight overhead, an infinite room with stars for walls and ceiling and a smooth grey floor of cloud. And into this room, from different directions, the ponderous yet graceful liners of the air approached, the low throbbing of their engines making themselves felt at a level seemingly far below that of true hearing, like the vibrations from the deepest notes of the largest pipes of a tremendous organ. For a moment Sorin wondered if the organist of the Castle Church were practicing. He gazed down, but saw no lights shining out from behind the tall narrow windows. The church was still and silent.

Mechanically, Sorin unslung his binoculars and carefully laid them on the floor. He wondered if he still had the same slightly unfocussed look that he'd noticed in Rainer's pale blue eyes as they'd grinned and laughed while shaking hands at the station. Lereanu had commented on it once, saying that his son clearly spent as much time thinking and gazing up and out into infinity as he did down at his collection of stamps and aviation photographs. Sorin felt Rainer tapping on his shoulder. He turned to face him. The droning sounds suddenly became real. "Sorin, they are coming! And both at once!" Rainer whispered. "Can't you hear—and feel them?"

The young men ran out onto the terrace. Overhead the cloud was still a monotonous sheet of dirty grey, but

A Flowering Wound

the unmistakable noise of aero engines grew louder every second. "They must be barely above the clouds!" Sorin shouted. "Perhaps their altimeters aren't working properly."

Behind them in the tower room the radio hissed and bubbled before the sounds were cut off when the headphones were plugged in again. "I can hear them—I think it's the *Friedrich*," someone shouted. Sorin and Rainer found themselves in a dilemma. They were torn by the desire to listen, to stand by the radio and be told what was being said by the crew overhead, and the wish to be on the terrace and hear the passage of the airships above the clouds, and not let pass even the slightest possibility that they would be able to see something.

Sorin rushed over to the radio, picked up the spare headphones, and put them on. "Yes, it's the *Friedrich der Grosse*," he said after listening for a few moments. Then he looked perplexed. "This is strange. They are saying that they can't see the *Oktober*. They have worked out their position and they know they're over Steaua de Munte, but they say there is no sign of the Russian airship. They're going to throttle back and circle around."

"That can't be right!" Rainer said. "You heard the noise outside. There are two airships up there."

Gabriel Lereanu followed his glance at the open door to the terrace, and went out. He heard the low buzzing and roaring of engines coming from two directions and gradually converging on each other close by, but out of sight above the layer of cloud. He shouted to the others inside the room. "Yes, I'm sure there're two of them. I can definitely make out two sources of noise. They don't quite sound the same. The *Friedrich* crew must be looking in the wrong direction, or the navigator on the *Oktober* got their position all wrong."

"Try and get the Russian airship," Sorin said to one of the radio men.

Twilight of the Airships

"Yes, here it is," he replied after a few seconds. "This must be them. I know Russian when I hear it." He handed Sorin the headphones, who passed them to Rainer.

"I don't believe this," Rainer said. "The *Oktober* says that they're in the rendezvous position and they can't see the *Friedrich*. And they're not being very, ah, nice about it!"

The noise of the airships' engines now penetrated the tower room. It was as if they were being run just outside and above the windows. The air vibrated. Then there was a series of flashes, like lightning. Lereanu turned back to the little terrace. He braced himself for the thunderclaps, but none came. The cloud layer overhead was still dark and unbroken, but now it was lit from horizon to horizon every few seconds by blinding flashes of light that remained visible even when Lereanu closed his eyes and tried to blink them away, shaking his head. Then he made out two elongated shapes, two slim shadows black against the dark cloud, moving slowly towards each other. With a jolt of astonishment he remembered that the airships were as large as ocean liners. Their positions coincided with the noise of the engines, although their buzzing and roaring now seemed to fill the entire sky. There were more flashes, followed by low rumbling and a red glow. The cloud layer flickered like a faulty arc light. Then Lereanu was reminded of fragments of burning paper, their edges twisting and smouldering from orange to red as they crumbled away into darkness. He almost laughed out loud in relief. Surely it really was only a thunderstorm that he was looking at! But no, that wasn't right. What was taking place above the clouds had nothing to do with the weather up there.

"The *Friedrich* still can't see anything," Sorin said. "They say all there is are stars and cloud. No, wait—someone's now shouting about the searchlights!"

160

A Flowering Wound

"And the *Oktober* crew are still saying that the *Friedrich* is nowhere in sight," Rainer said. "The captain's yelling about wasting time and fuel with this part of the flight. Ah, there's someone else shouting now." Rainer smiled. "The captain is now saying that naturally he is eager and willing to pursue the course decided by the correct authorities. But he's still asking where the *Friedrich* actually is, and if someone else would care to open his eyes and take a look around."

"There are no searchlights! What's that man talking about?" Lereanu called from the doorway. Below, as far as he could see, everyone in the city seemed to be oblivious to anything out of the ordinary occurring over them. On the ground it was still an ordinary April night. All was tranquil. The headlights of traffic moving along the boulevards, the streetlights and the lights of houses and illuminated shops formed a glimmering, twinkling forest.

Sorin said, "He is saying that he remembers flying in the Zeppelin air raids on London and the searchlights, but the English only used them when the sky was clear. Now he's cursing the ability of Russian airship navigators!" Sorin closed his eyes as he continued to monitor the agitated voices.

"So much for the camaraderie of the air," one of the radio men remarked.

Suddenly the tower room was filled with a lurid crimson glow. Flashes of white, yellow, and orange flared and washed over the walls. The radio men rushed to the windows, and Lereanu went back out onto the terrace. The cloud layer was on fire, a swirling and flickering vortex of molten colours. The sound of the engines kept changing pitch. The shapes of the airships changed direction. Then they were joined by other and different shapes, much smaller and moving faster, like birds mobbing an intruder. Lereanu breathed in hot and smoky air, and coughed. His eyes watered. "Those are not the right shapes!" he shouted. He clutched the

161

railing, swaying slightly as he held on to it. There were more flashes and rumblings, and a long drawn-out roar like a building collapsing. The din of the engines swelled and then faded again.

"The *Oktober* says the ground must be on fire!" Rainer shouted over the clamour. "He says there must be a sea of flames beneath them, below the cloud. The cloud layer is red. They're saying that they must be flying over Hell. They sound frightened. They're not talking about the Germans anymore."

The small shapes vanished as quickly as they had appeared. Lereanu watched the two great shadows continue moving towards each other. He moaned in helpless despair, but couldn't look away. Then he thought he saw the shapes collide. For a moment he thought it was more of a merging, but that could not be. He hunched his shoulders as he waited for the explosion and the showers of flaming debris that must come plummeting through the cloud and shower onto the town. The noise of the engines altered again and the two different sounds became distinct once more. The vast and vague shapes he had been tracking were now separate and moving away from each other. More concussions boomed and reverberated through the air, and the clouds still flashed and flickered, but no airships flaring like torches plunged to earth. There were no writhing human forms falling swiftly before being extinguished. No gobbets of flame dripped down to scatter destruction and terror.

Sorin tore off his headphones and pushed his knuckles into his eyes. He saw again the clean and light aluminium interiors: the empty corridors and cabins of the airship. Sunlight flooded in through the observation windows. In the near-silence of the flight the airship overtook fleecy white clouds. Sorin was aware of the stupendous volume of hydrogen filling the gasbags that surrounded the tiny rooms and corridors. And then the blinding light and the

A Flowering Wound

searing heat, the frenzied roar of straining, bursting engines, the splintering walkways and melting metal, with the floor suddenly tilting at a crazy angle—

"I've lost the *Oktober*," Rainer said. "It's gone, they've stopped transmitting!"

Lereanu staggered into the room. "I don't know what's happening," he gasped. He looked up at the ceiling, as if he could see through it to the tumult in the sky. He tilted his head back and shook his fist in the air. "You're both wrong! You're getting it wrong! What are you doing? You're not in the right place. Get back on your courses! There's nothing happening down here, we're not doing anything!"

Sorin dropped the headphones and darted over to his father, steadying him and guiding him to a seat. Lereanu sagged down in the chair and seemed to faint, but almost immediately opened his eyes again. He straightened up a little and looked around him in horror, before seeming to realise that he was out of it, after all. He grasped his son's hand. Rainer walked slowly over to them and sat down on the floor, resting his head against the back of the chair. He rubbed at his eyes again. They brimmed with tears, which he wiped away with his sleeve.

The radio operators had remained with their equipment, and had resumed listening. "I've got the *Friedrich der Grosse* on here," one said. "From what I can understand they're saying the searchlights have been turned off, but it's as if Steaua de Munte were ablaze. They are still convinced their position is correct. They say that the clouds are burning, smouldering. They are going to gain height and get away from here, whether or not they spot the *Oktober* in the next few minutes."

Sorin bent and kissed his father on the forehead, then remained with him, holding his hand. Rainer returned to the radio and donned his headphones again. He began to listen intently. "The *Oktober* is back too," he said. "They

163

Twilight of the Airships

don't know what's happened. But they're going to increase speed and height and continue the flight. They are going to radio home for further instructions what to say about the rendezvous not having taken place."

The sound of the airships' engines returned to what it had been when they had first come into range. They faded away as their distance increased. The tower room grew dim again, with the only illumination being provided by the lamps. After a few minutes the radio men nodded and switched off the set and began to disconnect the aerial. Rainer stood up and went out onto the terrace. Overhead the clouds were once more a uniform dark grey, smooth and silent. Lereanu got to his feet and shakily followed Rainer outside. Sorin joined them. They breathed in the cool and fresh night air gratefully.

Lereanu shook his head, as if trying to shake away what he had glimpsed in his vision. Against skies of daylight, darkness, and bloody sunset, sleek silver airships were wreathed in haloes of fire, and their crews and passengers danced in pentecosts of flame. But as they blackened in the furnace, their open mouths were not calling out praise in many tongues, but breaking out in rending screams. "I heard one last thing," Lereanu said. "I heard a voice speaking. It was in English. It was distorted, it sounded like it was coming from thousands of miles away. I couldn't make sense of what it said, but I know it was dreadful." But he wouldn't tell them anything more.

⁊⧉

Gabriel Lereanu left the display in his shop window untouched for as long as he could, until the sold merchandise was collected or had to be sent to its purchasers. Finally he spent an entire two days planning and creating a completely new display. He removed the posters and gave them

164

A Flowering Wound

to Sorin, who rolled them back up into their protective cardboard tubes and put them away in one of the storage cabinets in his room.

The publicity surrounding the airships' completion of their flights was intense. The world of aviation and the supporters of airship travel and commerce in particular hailed them as great achievements and their crews as intrepid pioneers. They were fêted by the leaders and citizens of the countries over which they flew and cheered by tremendous crowds in the cities where their great grey ships had moored, as they were driven through the streets on their way to banquets held in their honour. Decorations were bestowed. Even so, the news of the failure of the airships' rendezvous had quickly spread. The German and Soviet governments released almost identical statements regretting that adverse weather conditions had suddenly and unexpectedly sprung up over Transylvania and prevented the airships being navigated to their planned positions. Nothing to the contrary was printed in any newspaper or aviation journal; the celebratory newsreels did not mention or show anything of those sections of the airships' milestone flights.

Rainer stayed on with the Lereanu family for another week before he left to rejoin his friends for the final part of their Danube trip, and during that time both he and Sorin followed the remainder of the flights with undiminished interest. Like the airship posters pushed far back into the black depths of Sorin's cupboard, both men tried to hold down what they had seen and heard and yet slam the door shut on it. By an unspoken mutual consent they tried to ignore and forget their experiences and memories of the night the airships flew over Steaua de Munte.

To some extent it worked. The airships returned home and the world's attention moved on. Sorin was surprised to receive the letters and cards that he had arranged for the

Twilight of the Airships

Friedrich der Grosse and the *Oktober* to carry with them on their flights. Those that Lereanu advertised and offered for sale quickly sold, while Sorin packed several envelopes covered with the special postage stamps and now bearing unique postmarks, labels, and endorsements into a tin box which he stored in the same cupboard as the posters.

The Soviet government announced no further flights for the *Oktober* or its sister ships. While the *Friedrich der Grosse* was being checked over, the *Graf Zeppelin* and *Hindenburg* maintained their regular commercial flight schedules. When Sorin heard the news that the *Hindenburg* had exploded while mooring at Lakehurst he was as shocked and appalled by the disaster as anyone. But it wasn't only the loss of life that shook him. He knew that it could so easily have been far greater. Sorin had the conviction that the catastrophe also represented the end of an all-too brief age and the loss of something great and wonderful, where human beings had met and overcome challenges of engineering, technology, and exploration. Mere people—tiny, limited—had created the giant airships that had solemnly sailed the skies of the world and raised the eyes of a generation to the heavens, and perhaps to the possibilities beyond.

Throughout the world all the remaining airships were grounded. Germany cancelled its plan for a successor to the *Friedrich der Grosse*, and the Soviet Union broke up its airship fleet and reassigned their crews and technical personnel. Sorin came to feel an overwhelming sense of sadness and grief for the greater loss. He felt guilty and ashamed, and said nothing to his father or anyone else, because he didn't want to be misunderstood. There were awkward times when Sorin thought that his father wanted to say something to him, but he never did; and Sorin didn't feel it was right to intrude by encouraging him. But Sorin did confide his thoughts in a letter to Rainer, who replied with sympathy

A Flowering Wound

and understanding, telling his friend that he would now have no choice but to seek to use his qualifications in a different field of aviation to that of airships.

One evening in early summer Sorin and his father went to watch a film at the Kino Mitteleuropa. The tall curving façade of the cinema reminded Sorin of an airship at dock, pressing down and intimidating him by its scale. Afterwards, as they stood in the bright and shiny foyer, Sorin noticed that his father's hands were shaking. Lereanu thrust them into the pockets of his jacket, and said brusquely that he wished to have a drink in the cinema bar. The two men sat in silence with their glasses of plum brandy. Sorin waited for his father to speak. Lereanu swallowed his drink and signalled for another.

"Sorin, do you remember that night of the airships, when we were at the top of the tower, and I said that I'd heard something that I couldn't make sense of?"

"Yes. I remember that. I don't think I'll ever forget what happened."

"I won't either. But I did hear something, and I'm still far from sure about what it really means. Now I'm going to tell you. I've not told your mother or anyone else." Lereanu paused, and drank more brandy. "It was the newsreel we just saw. Why do they keep showing it? It brought it all back. The bit when they showed the film of the *Hindenburg* blowing up, with the commentary from that American newsman. When I saw it at the time I thought I could make the memory go away, but I haven't been able to. That night—I shouted at the airships to go away, didn't I? They were wrong and I told them to go away. Now it's all come back to me again. I heard that sobbing voice, the distorted sounds, the terror, the drawn-out agonies, the loss, all the emotions." Lereanu gazed at Sorin in anguish. "And I hear one cry, over and over again: *Oh, the humanity!*"

Under the Sun

I spent much of my earliest childhood imagining that the entire country, if not the world, was like the street where we lived. And now I wonder if I hadn't been on to something. There are times when I come to think that the suburb in which I've ended up—if not the road or my house—is, quite possibly, the world.

I was born and brought up in suburban Middlesex, that county curled around London to the west and north, and where, decades earlier, the urban had almost completely overwhelmed the rural. There was no longer a mix of town and country, but a layer of buildings and open spaces often thinly spread over a landscape where natural boundaries had long since ceased to count, but where evidence of the past was still visible to those who knew how to look. Old houses and walls, trees, scraps of hedges, fragments of fields—these sometimes still survived in the midst of the newer order. And as the scars of urban sprawl healed, the new pattern of streets became tree-lined and shady, gardens and parks bloomed, and the freshly-built houses, shops, cinemas, and pubs mellowed and lost their harsh edges. In turn they became part of the transformed landscape, a combination of grass and trees and brick and tarmac fused into something else entirely.

Of course I had soon discovered that not everywhere was like my part of Ealing. That kindled my interest in other places. Eventually I started collecting books of travel

A Flowering Wound

reminiscences, photographs, and maps. I became an experienced armchair traveller. The world was a place for amazement and awe, and I also saw no reason why my part of London should be any different. By the time I left school and went to work, I was in effect two people inhabiting one body and leading almost completely separate lives. I also enthusiastically joined my friends in having girlfriends, planning buying our first cars, and in looking forward to being able to go drinking—legally.

Soon I got married, and we bought a house. We had our own careers, and decided against raising a family. We had each other; we had interests in common as well as those we pursued separately. During all this time I explored the hidden places and byways of West London, seeking out and accumulating books and maps delineating the places that so fascinated me. In my mind I journeyed near and far—and all the faster for travelling alone. My wife would say that it was as good as being in two places at once. And as the years passed I thought that I must have got away with it. Later she said I never really ever wanted nor needed any company.

❧

When it became clear that our marriage was over, I had agreed to the sale of our house. I immediately started to look for another place in Ealing or close by. Someone at work had suggested Turnham Park.

One blustery Saturday in October I had been bursting with nervous energy so I picked up a street atlas and walked. Even without the map I could have told when I reached Turnham Park. The streets started to curve and were lined with old trees. Terraced houses were replaced by houses standing in their own gardens. Yellowing leaves blew down across lawns and the open space of The Green. A parade

Under the Sun

of red brick shops glowed in the low sun, and small white houses shone out against bare grey trees and the empty blue sky. I wandered around for an hour or so, breathing in all the stimulating smells of damp grass and dead leaves—and everything that went with the decaying year. As I walked home again I thought that if I could find a little house in Turnham Park I would be able to make the new start I was being forced into somewhat more palatable. Turnham Park was a defined area in the vast and chaotic wonder that was London; more than anything else at that time I craved definitions, boundaries, and a refuge from chaos until I was ready and able to confront and interact with it once more.

I moved to Turnham Park at the beginning of January. As the removals van drove away I slammed the front door closed and leaned back against it. That fitted my mood. Now the divorce had been made absolute I wanted nothing more than to retreat into a place I could call home, to gather all my possessions around me. At times I had thought this was perhaps an over-materialistic approach, but it felt right and necessary as my life came apart and the only thing I had to look forward to was repairing it.

The house was cold. Although I wore a thick jacket and was still warm from driving back and forth from Ealing with the items I hadn't trusted to the removals firm, I knew I would soon also feel the January chill. Outside, the low grey sky was already darkening, and streetlights were coming on. Lights were being switched on in rooms and curtains drawn against the advancing dusk. Luckily there had been vacant possession, and I had been able to arrange for curtains to be hung, the heating to be overhauled, and basic redecorating to be done.

I loathe the cold and I don't like the thought of being observed. Still bundled in my jacket and avoiding the unplaced furniture and ziggurats of boxes as best I could,

A Flowering Wound

I went through the house—unfamiliar territory as yet—drawing curtains and turning on lights. Bare walls were harsh under the overhead lighting, and the rooms called out to have their echoes absorbed by my possessions. I switched on the heating, too. That afternoon I would make one more trip outside, to the supermarket in the High Road, before starting on the task of putting together a new home.

As the house began to grow warm and come alive I returned to the hall and leaned back against the front door again. The radiators and pipes gurgled softly and floors creaked and groaned. No doubt I would grow used to all these sounds: they would become familiar and predictable. I pressed my palms back against the painted wood. A strange house is a new country. I had closed its door behind me. When I went through it again in a moment it would be as an inhabitant of Turnham Park: an explorer of unfamiliar territory in a place where I now had a right to be.

These thoughts and others like them were a comfort and anchor. Even so, in reality Turnham Park wasn't, of course, a completely unexplored and alien region for me. I was born in Ealing and had lived most of my life there. I worked in Park Royal. I knew where Turnham Park was, even though I had never been there except when delays on the North Circular Road led me to penetrate its quiet streets, driving through on my way to somewhere else.

❧

During the first weeks of the New Year I settled in and arranged my furniture and possessions. I sold my car: there was no garage and I didn't like the idea of parking it on the street, even though my new neighbours said there shouldn't be any problems. So my car was a possession I let go, even as I anticipated taking up life among all my remaining ones.

Under the Sun

There was a Tube station by The Green; several bus routes passed through Turnham Park or ran along the main roads that looped around the suburb like a moat. It was easy to get to work, and I could even walk part or all of the way if I had to.

By the middle of February, as the days slowly lengthened, I was walking several miles a day in the crisp air, and felt all the better for it. Friends at work made positive comments about my leaner appearance and growing ruddiness. A tentative contentment began to settle over me. It was only as I switched on my computer that I noticed the scattering of cards on other people's desks, and realised it was Valentine's Day. It had been our anniversary, and for weeks I had been dreading it. But I realised that recently I had forgotten to dread it. The thought of not always having someone present, of not always being accompanied, no longer worried me. That evening as I walked home through the sunset streets, weaving my way as much as possible through side and residential roads, I smiled to myself and began to seriously hope that the coming spring would not only bring the earth's rebirth but mine as well.

When it became warm enough I opened the French windows in the sitting room and kept them open. The garden was tiny, and the shadows gathered early, but I'd had the idea of filling the paved area with large pots of lavender. The scent of lavender brought back childhood memories of warm days playing in the garden or running along our road with friends, as well as the smell of my grandmother's clothes stored in the wardrobe allocated to her when she'd come to live with us. In the dusk the years sometimes seemed to fall away and regrets and sorrows fade into the dimming background. I would sit in an armchair with a strong lamp behind me while I read a travel book or pored over an old atlas or street plan. As the last light

A Flowering Wound

drained out of the sky I would switch off the lamp and sit in the gloom. Breathing in the perfume of the lavender with the tang of damp stone underlying it, I would look around the room at the blank rectangles of framed maps, and the bookcases standing out against the pale walls like the hulking bastions of a fortress of the mind.

As spring advanced my sense of equipoise grew until it often seemed that the events that had brought me to Turnham Park had happened to someone else. Of course, there were still times when I gave in to self-pity or anger (or both). I developed nodding acquaintances at the Park Tavern on those evenings I went there for a few drinks. But it seemed to me that wounds were fast healing, and I would then also be better able to contemplate wounds I must have caused.

※

I was used to thinking of London suburbs as places where beauty and enchantment could be found. For obvious reasons these considerations hadn't always been uppermost in my mind over recent months, although at unexpected moments the glimpse of an ivy-covered brick wall, the silhouette of chimneys against the churning clouds of an apocalyptic sunset, or the sight of a front garden with snowdrops nodding in the chill of a breezy dusk would cause me to stand away from myself, however briefly, in a reverie of wonder and delight. As I sat in my armchair at home I was glad that I hadn't lost the ability to lose myself in that way—or that it hadn't been taken from me.

Spring in Turnham Park was a riot of colour: trees flaming into blossom and hedges flaring up into emerald ramparts. Even so, the intensity of the spring and early summer was only a prologue. We settled down into a

Under the Sun

prolonged heatwave. I invoked my right to work flexible hours, and arrived as early as possible, having threaded my way through all but silent streets even then shimmering with heat-haze under the intense power of the rising sun. When I was asked to work over a couple of weekends, I was happy enough to do so. After work I invariably caught the bus home, rather than expose myself to the fierce heat and sunlight of the afternoon.

In the late evening I would wander around Turnham Park, choosing roads where the old trees made shady tunnels in which faint and fleeting drafts of slightly cooler air could sometimes be felt. The smell of newly cut grass was everywhere. It was as if it were now only possible to experience the suburb by muted or indirect sunlight. The full light of the sun near the meridian would blast away all sight, all colours and sensations, leaving only irresistible heat and whiteness impossible to look at. I was protected from all that by being safely in the office during those hours. For all I knew the heat melted Turnham Park into a new form each noon, before it flowed together again and I found it there once more, outwardly as I had left it, but entirely renewed.

The heatwave eased. I began three weeks of holiday on the day fantastic storms and torrential rain lowered the temperature and cleansed the air. On the second day I still woke up very early. I looked out onto a Turnham Park that seemed as if it had just been created. I walked out into my little garden, making sure the lavender was not drowning in its pots. After breakfast I decided to take the Tube into central London. As I strolled across The Green I noted that the grass was already dry.

On the third day I rested. As lunchtime approached I realised I had almost no food in the house. I also remembered my imaginings about Turnham Park at noon. Although the heatwave had faded somewhat, another period of very hot

A Flowering Wound

and relentlessly sunny weather seemed to be taking hold. The sky was clear and deep; everything was bathed in strong sunshine. Keeping to any shade I could find, I wandered in the direction of the High Road.

In some ways seeing Turnham Park in the full glare of noon was to see it for the first time. At first glance houses and trees and hedges looked as if they'd been cut out and painted in particularly garish and glaring colours; light and colour radiated out as powerfully as heat. Flowerbeds were pools of flame. I felt that too much light was trying to force itself into my eyes and flood all my senses. Putting on my sunglasses didn't provide much relief. I walked slowly, trying not to get too hot. As my eyes accustomed themselves, some range of subtlety and gradation of colour and shading returned to the scene. It was too bright to do more than glance up above roof level. The sunlight revealed without mercy the weathered brick of the aging houses, the hazy edges of trees and shrubs, the slowly softening roads and pavements.

Although I had remembered my sunglasses I didn't have a cap or hat to wear. On the way back home I resigned myself to getting thoroughly overheated. The sun was at my back, casting a minimal shadow before me. Ahead of me the street seemed endless. I decided to turn into the next street on my side of Wadham Road and circle round back to my road, staying in the shade as much as possible. I was confident that I now knew my way around Turnham Park well enough. In any case, even if I ended up staying out in the sun longer than I intended, there was no way I could get lost in such a small and defined area as the suburb.

I came to a junction. But instead of turning in to the street I stopped. My bag of shopping seemed to double in weight and every drop of sweat that it seemed possible for my head and neck to produce began to trickle down my back. I started to walk around the corner. Now the

Under the Sun

new street ran on in front of me, with plenty of shade cast over the pavement by the high hedges and tall shrubs surrounding the houses. But there was something in my way: it was as if I were gazing at the road through a sheet of glass, or looking at a picture. I stopped again. Standing in a patch of shade, I put down my shopping and waited for my body to cool down. I looked around. I couldn't see a street sign—but sometimes they did get obscured or even completely hidden by untrimmed hedges. I was sure—I *knew*—that I must have seen the street before, but if so, it looked different in the overpowering glare of the sun. I was sure I knew exactly where in Turnham Park I was standing, yet I felt I was in danger of getting lost. I stood there a little longer until the sweat had dried on my back and I felt calmer. Then I picked up my bag and continued on home. I wasn't going to enter that other street.

Later, lying stretched out on the sofa in my sitting room, with the French windows open and lavender in the air, I thought back over my experience. Outside, the sun drenched the garden and all Turnham Park in a hammering deluge of light. In the room it was dim, as if I were still wearing my sunglasses. Bookshelves, maps and pictures were indistinct as I tried to focus my eyes on them.

I had deliberately decided not to get out a street atlas and follow my route on a map of Turnham Park. Streets of old houses don't appear out of nothing. It must have been because it was my first summer in Turnham Park: I hadn't seen the suburb before at that time of year and time of day. And it was possible that I had become slightly disorientated in the heat and glare. Eventually I drowsed through the rest of the afternoon.

A Flowering Wound

❧

The next morning I awoke groggy and tired. Perhaps my experience of the street had affected me more than I realised. The sky was vacant: a metallic and dusty blue with the sun a searing eye. This early in the day everything seemed to be blooming and truly alive—except me. I wondered if I was already becoming bored with living in Turnham Park. I reflected that the circumstances which had led me to move there had not been of my choice—even though in some measure I had borne some of the responsibility. But no: I liked the quiet suburb, I loved my small house. I had spent time and money making it into a home; I had invested it with the things I cared for and with myself. There was no question but that moving forward with my life involved remaining where I had decided to live. And yet, it seemed to me, some other factor had now entered and was beginning to make itself felt.

I waited until noon before going out for a walk. This time I put on an old cap as well as my sunglasses. I wore the thinnest white cotton shirt I could find, but when I left the house it was still like trying to crash through a solid wall of heat. The next sensation was even more physical. At first I put it down to my body reacting to the high temperature and sudden flood of light. As I closed the garden gate behind me I had the sense that someone was with me. Someone had left the house and slipped through the gate ahead of me during the few seconds it had been open. I blinked rapidly and shook my head, as if trying to dislodge something in my eye.

As I walked slowly in the direction of The Green, I stayed in the shade as much as I possibly could. The pavements were almost deserted. Snatches of music and conversation drifted from the open windows of the house on the corner.

Under the Sun

In the distance a bus was a hot red smear. The upper windows of the buildings in the High Road glittered. I stopped at the Park Tavern for a sandwich and a pint. The doors were propped open, their small panels of coloured glass dull and grimy. As I entered the murky bar I stepped a little to one side to let someone come in past me, but no-one did.

The sense of someone keeping close to me returned after I left the pub and went back out into the blazing afternoon. In the High Road there was a lot of traffic and the shops were busy, as usual. My sunglasses kept slipping, and as I stopped to push them up into place again I would glance around, but I couldn't make out whether any of the people out and about in the heat of the day were shadowing me. It just felt like it. I told myself that I was imagining things, that it was the heat—but the feeling persisted.

Back in Turnham Park a cyclist brushed past me on the pavement as I strolled into Wadham Road. The momentary breeze was welcome, but left me still feeling uneasy. I kept looking behind me, but the pavement was empty. As I approached the corner of the street I had the impression that there was someone standing on the kerb ahead of me, as if waiting to cross the road. I took my sunglasses off and rubbed my eyes, but there was still nobody there. My cap was damp with sweat. I thought about looking for the street sign, but the idea of pushing my hands into the garden hedge hiding it held no appeal. I was now facing into the long empty street. It dwindled away in flickering perspective, insubstantial in the sunlight. A garden gate slammed shut. Now there was a man striding towards me on the pavement. The slabs were uneven and seemed to tilt under his feet as he trod on them, avoiding the lines where they joined. I pulled at my sunglasses when I thought I saw his face clearly—and then the world twisted at an angle and blurred as I fell.

A Flowering Wound

I must have been able to walk aided, but I remembered nothing of how I came to find myself lying in a deckchair in a little gazebo entirely hidden from the road by the hedge and fence surrounding the garden of the house on the corner. It was shady and quite cool. A damp towel—not the first, it seemed—was being placed on my burning forehead.

"You don't seem to have hurt yourself," I heard a voice say. "You folded up and fell so cleanly, as if you'd been practising. It was amazing. You're not an actor or stunt man, are you?"

All I could mumble was, "What happened?"

"Sorry, I didn't mean to make light of it. You fainted, just as I was coming out of my garden. You just went down, folded up on the pavement. I saw it all."

I opened my eyes. Sitting forward on another deckchair and leaning towards me was a man of about my age and build. His forehead was creased in concern, but he quickly broke into an easy smile. "Like I said, I don't think you hit your head or anything, but I'd still go to a doctor if I were you."

"But you're not me," I snapped. As soon as I had spoken, I reconsidered: "Listen, I'm sorry. That was really rude of me. I'm glad you happened to be there. Thank you for helping me. I'm really grateful."

"That's all right. Perhaps you're still in a bit of shock or something. It's like a furnace, out in the sun."

He gave me a glass of water mixed with melting cubes of ice. I gulped it down as fast as I could.

"This has never happened before," I said. "I was only on my way back from the shops."

"Were you going to visit someone round here? Just before you fainted you seemed to be looking along the street, right past where I was, as if you'd spotted someone you knew. But I'd only just seen you, so I might've got that wrong.

Under the Sun

I can walk with you to where you were going, if you like. Just to make sure you're okay getting there."

I didn't want to tell him why I had been on the corner. Even though he had helped me, he was, after all, still a complete stranger, and I didn't want to give him an excuse to walk home with me and see where I lived.

"That's all right, thanks," I said. "I'll be fine. I'm feeling much better now. Like you said, it must've been a touch of the sun." I made myself laugh. "I'll have to get a Panama hat. Mad dogs and Englishmen, and all that!"

"Well, if you're sure."

He walked with me to the garden gate and let me out, back on to the road. I smiled and nodded, and walked slowly back the way I had come, trying to conjure an air of nonchalance I didn't feel. This time I had no feelings of being accompanied. By the time I got home I was sweating heavily and feeling very thirsty. I dropped into my armchair and dozed. When I woke up a couple of hours later I realised that neither my rescuer nor I had introduced ourselves, and I hadn't discovered the name of that street, let alone entered and walked along it.

My discourtesy to the man who had helped me bothered me. I didn't want to speak to him again straight away, but even though I had apologised at the time I wanted to make amends, and sooner rather than later. Feeling old-fashioned and self-conscious, I wrote a short note of thanks, apologising and inviting my new acquaintance to join me for a drink and meal at the Park Tavern—later that evening, if it would be convenient. I tried to keep the tone light and hopefully not open to being misconstrued in any way. Then I made myself walk straight to his house.

It was still very hot. Although the sun had now moved into the west it was as powerful as ever, boring into everything and painting everywhere in a deep yellow layer of

A Flowering Wound

light. I kept my eyes on the pavement as much as I could, only glancing up when a kerb came into view or I sensed someone was coming in the other direction. Once again I had no feeling of someone being with me, for which I was grateful. I wondered if everything I had felt really could be put down to having exposed myself too much to the sun.

In Wadham Road a teenager was delivering copies of the local free newspaper, and I offered him a pound coin and asked him to put my note through the letterbox with the paper. He took the money and did as I asked. Retracing my steps in the glowing afternoon I was back home again within a few minutes.

As I approached the Park Tavern I thought about sitting at one of the tables in the fenced-off space outside, but they were crowded and I hoped it would be slightly cooler inside. I bought a drink and found a table. As my eyes got accustomed to the welcome dimness I studied the food menu, but found I wasn't hungry. All the windows and doors were open. Here and there bars of golden light thrust into the room.

I noticed my guest threading his way through the tables, in and out of the light. I stood up to greet him, and we shook hands, introducing ourselves—properly, this time. His name was David—my middle name, as I quickly told him. Then I felt embarrassed at giving so much away so soon. He said he wasn't hungry, having eaten earlier, so we simply sat there sipping our beer.

"How long have you lived in Turnham Park?" David asked.

"Only since the beginning of the year," I said. Then I found myself explaining why I'd moved there, about my marriage and divorce, what I thought about Turnham Park, and my growing sense of wellbeing and confidence. He nodded as I spoke, putting me at my ease in the same way a practised interviewer or counsellor does. I wanted to shut up and let him speak, ask him about himself in response,

Under the Sun

but I couldn't stop talking. I started to describe the sense of unease I'd felt when I'd been out walking, and how I'd felt somehow shadowed. I was sure I was making a fool of myself, being rude and thoughtless all over again, but I ploughed on regardless. Then, at last, I ground to a halt. To cover my shame I quickly got up to buy another round as David looked on with what I hoped was real sympathy.

For the rest of the evening I think I regained my awareness of social norms. David had also grown up in Ealing, and soon we were reminiscing about places we remembered and how they'd changed. And he seemed to understand and share the attraction I felt for living in a place like Turnham Park. It seemed special for him too. Then his phone bleeped and he read the message.

"It's the wife, wondering when I'll be back. I told her what happened and that I was meeting you for a quick drink." He looked at his phone. "It hasn't been a quick drink, has it?" he said.

I shook my head. "I enjoyed it. Thanks again for helping me, and thanks for coming. And thank you for putting up with me rambling on like that, earlier."

"Alex, why don't you come round for lunch on Sunday? We've got some other friends coming, and Claire would love to meet you. We'll be eating out in the garden, if the weather's still fine."

Outside the pub we shook hands. I'd told David that I'd let him know about the lunch. I said I needed to buy some milk at the supermarket in the High Road, and walked off in the opposite direction to him. I didn't want him accompanying me for any distance, and I didn't want to go straight home. I felt a pang of jealousy about David having a wife. I knew how absurd that was, but nevertheless I felt it. I'd imagined us as being two free men, brothers in adversity. But any adversity now seemed to be solely on my side.

A Flowering Wound

Walking past The Green, under the railway bridge and the short distance to the High Road was to leave one world for an entirely different one. The main road was still busy with traffic: car headlights moved slowly, stopping and starting as traffic lights changed. It was still very warm, and the pavements were crowded with people leaving pubs and waiting for buses. I heard the constant subdued gabble of voices discussing what I was sure must be nothing import-ant. But at least they were talking to friends, companions. I walked on past the supermarket, hands in my pocket. I had worn a fairly smart shirt—one slightly too thick for such hot and close weather. My collar was damp and sweat trickled down my back.

Above the bright groove of the High Road the sky wasn't fully dark. The last daylight was stained with endless light of the night-time city. I hadn't paid full attention to where I was walking, and I jostled someone standing at a corner. I apologised and turned into the street, walking back into Turnham Park. Within moments it was quieter and darker. I looked around hastily, to check the man I'd bumped into wasn't following me. The street was empty. I was alone. And I felt alone again—even as just then I think I would've welcomed the sense of being accompanied, as I had been before, even though it was by a presence I couldn't define or perhaps didn't want to attempt to.

❧

Although I was sure I'd talked far too much and been socially awkward, I still felt that I'd made a new friend in David. As men from similar backgrounds and with many experiences in common, and both beginning the journey into middle age, I felt we had found a mutual kinship. I was looking forward to developing it. Male bonding and all

Under the Sun

that: I'd never taken it seriously. If anything I'd treated it as a mawkish phenomenon found in films: not as something for me. But now I was on my own again I realised that all along I had been missing out on friendship—and I meant friendship, not just a work colleague to go to the pub with—whether male or female. I certainly wasn't ready to get into dating, so the prospect of a close male friend with whom I could discuss men's issues and do things that men of our age are supposed to like to do, became more and more appealing.

For the rest of the week I didn't leave the house. I wanted to stay out of the sun. I called David to accept the invitation to Sunday lunch, and even made a very weak joke about making up the numbers at an attempt by him at match-making. I spent those hot and sticky days in my shady sitting room lounging on the sofa watching films or reading about Antarctica. The French windows were open from early morning to past dusk, and the smell of lavender pervaded the house. I recalled that the lavender in my garden was just about the only thing I hadn't talked to David about.

At lunch, as soon as the introductions were out of the way, the continuing scorching weather became the main topic of conversation. Apart from David and his wife there was one other married couple, and another single man. He had never been married and said he liked being on his own. Any thoughts on my part—whether seriously entertained or not—about match-making were also unfounded. I was relieved on all counts. We were all much the same age and from the same background: we remembered the same places and events. I don't think I said anything stupid and I certainly didn't drink too much of the various dry white wines the guests had brought and which had immediately been put in the fridge to chill. I thought the meal went

A Flowering Wound

well. I was part of a gathering of decent people who were good acquaintances or contacts, and quite likely to become good friends if I were to see more of them. But there were moments of agitation—which I tried to suppress—when I felt a nagging sense of aloneness, even as I sat and talked and laughed. At those moments I felt myself to be an outsider, a fraud. If I had told them what I thought had really happened a few days before, I would expose the truth about myself: the emptiness I had been trying to hide and forget about.

The lunch drew towards its close. We updated the contacts on our phones and said we'd keep in touch and no doubt see each other around Turnham Park. I shook hands or air-kissed before walking away across the sun-drenched lawn to the garden gate. And then, as I stood on the pavement and the gate clicked shut behind me, I knew I was accompanied—at a distance. At the corner I turned and gazed along the length of the street. I saw someone walking away from me. I took off my sunglasses, and in the full unmediated glare the figure was still there, still indistinct, still receding. I caught the faintest hint of lavender in the sparkling air, but I was sure it didn't come from where I had just been. Out of sight of anybody else, I started to follow.

❧

Now that the first dewy coolness of autumn has arrived, the long hot summer seems as if it had never happened. Or perhaps it was someone else who sat at home by his open windows or wandered the streets of the suburb under that unrelenting sun. These days I have no reluctance in walking along that street. I know its name: it is easily visible, and David tells me it has never been allowed to become hidden. I have no reason not to believe him.

Under the Sun

Turnham Park is a maze, its streets endlessly curving and circling, flowing into the other coloured paths that lead out into the other, and tremendous, labyrinth that is London. I know the exits, and I can leave whenever I want to or have to. But when I don't have to go to work I usually stay within the bounds of the maze. When I don't want to be at home reading or tending the garden I enjoy wandering through the streets, sometimes with a purpose, but usually just because I can. It's easy.

I tell myself that I'm not actively seeking a companion, but am willing to grow in preparedness. I tell myself I hope that I might stumble across it—I can't quite bring myself to use a human pronoun or to choose—or that it might reveal itself once more. But that hope is accompanied by apprehension. Opportunities and chances are also challenges. There could be consequences in straying from the paths. And so I remain content to work and walk, to stay at home and to meet my few friends, to stay within the limits and not to look out too far—and certainly not to explore too deeply within.

Acknowledgments

The publisher and author would like to thank Meggan Kehrli for her cover design, Jason Zerrillo for his artwork, Jim Rockill for his proofreading, and Ken Mackenzie for typesetting this book.

❧

"A Glimpse of the City" was first published in
Cities and Thrones and Powers
(Les Editions de l'Oubli, 2013).

"Portrait in an Unfaded Photograph" was first published in *Cinnabar's Gnosis: A Homage to Gustav Meyrink*, edited by D. T. Ghetu (Ex Occidente Press, 2009).

"The Golden Mile" was first published in
All Is Full of Hell: A Panegyric for William Blake,
edited by Damian Murphy & D. T. Ghetu
(Mount Abraxas, 2017).

"Falling Into Stone" was first published in *Horror Uncut: Tales of Social Insecurity and Economic Unease*, edited by Joel Lane & Tom Johnstone (Gray Friar Press, 2014).

Acknowledgments

"Ziegler Against the World"
was first published in *Transactions of the Flesh:
A Homage to Joris-Karl Huysmans,*
edited by D. P. Watt & Peter Holman
(Zagava and Ex Occidente Press, 2013).

"A Flowering Wound" was first published in
Never Again: Weird Fiction Against Racism and Fascism,
edited by Allyson Bird & Joel Lane
(Grey Friar Press, 2010).

"We, the Rescued"
was first published in *Nightscript 3,*
edited by C. M. Muller (Chthonic Matter, 2017).

"The Man Ahead"
appears for the first time in this collection.

"Twilight of the Airships" was first published in
Cities and Thrones and Powers
(Les Editions de l'Oubli, 2013).

"Under the Sun"
appears for the first time in this collection.